LOVE IS INNOCENT

The Duke of Atherstone had been driven to a frenzy. Every debutante in London wanted to marry him. Their determined mothers had transformed all of England into a matrimonial obstacle course.

Fleeing to the safety of his yacht, the Duke set sail for Monte Carlo. But even the dissipated society of the gaming tables provided no respite: Atherstone's charmingly jaded mistress soon launched her own marital plans. Furious, the Duke pulled up anchor again, heading for Algiers.

Foolishly convinced that no eligible young lady was waiting to entrap him, the Duke allowed himself the luxury of admiring an exquisite young English girl on sale in the Algerian Slave Market. As he moved closer to appraise her beauty, the terrified girl looked straight into his eyes, whispering: "Save me . . . save me!"

Bantam Books by Barbara Cartland
Ask your bookseller for the books you have missed

Love
Is
Innocent

Barbara Cartland

BANTAM BOOKS
TORONTO · NEW YORK · LONDON

LOVE IS INNOCENT
A Bantam Book / November 1975

Bantam Books are published by Bantam Books, Inc. Its trade-
mark, consisting of the words "Bantam Books" and the por-
trayal of a bantam, is registered in the United States Patent
Office and in other countries. Marca Registrada. Bantam
Books, Inc., 666 Fifth Avenue, New York, New York 10019.

PRINTED IN THE UNITED STATES OF AMERICA

Author's Note

The traffic of young girls to North Africa continued all through the nineteenth century and is now, according to reliable reports, centered in Lebanon.

The arrangements of sales described in this book still take place in the brothels.

Every year hundreds of foolish young women answer advertisements or accept positions in cabarets, theatres, or dance-halls without being assured of a return ticket home.

That the majority are enticed into becoming drug addicts is known to the police of every European country.

Notre Dame de Laghet is exactly as I have described and the medallions I carry always with me have, I am convinced, protected me against many accidents.

Chapter One

1887

The Duke of Atherstone stood on the deck of the *Sea Lion* as his yacht steamed into the harbour of Algiers.

It was early in the morning and there was that strange, translucent light which in North Africa preludes the full force of the sun.

The bay with its terraces of dazzling white and the emerald hills in the background blending with the haze in the azure blue of the sea seemed almost unreal.

But the Duke had a frown on his forehead and his eyes were hard as he watched his yacht move slowly towards the Quay and saw the usual crowd beginning to congregate with the arrival of a new-comer.

He had slept little the night before and was still angry with the fury which had driven him down to the harbour at Monte Carlo, where he had ordered his Captain to put to sea immediately.

It was typical of the perfectly organised manner with which the Duke ran his life that everything was always ready for a change of mood or a quick decision.

In his numerous houses his servants needed no announcement of his arrival.

Three months might elapse before he revisited any one of them but when he did everything was exactly as he expected it to be.

He travelled without luggage for his clothes were duplicated in his various residences. Although his Secretary and his valet were part of his personal entourage

1

they had underlings to take their place should the Duke travel without them.

Already the Duke had the reputation of being a perfectionist, which was unusual in a man of thirty-four, and conscious of his own importance he ensured that his comfort was a first consideration with those he employed.

At the same time his life, which should have been without a cloud on the horizon, had unexpectedly run into a storm.

It was indeed a storm that had made him lose his temper the night before and which had brought him quite without forethought into the centuries-old port of Algiers.

It had been deservedly called the Garden of the Gods, but this did not lessen the frown on the Duke's face nor the hard line of his lips.

With a great deal of noise from the boatmen and sailors on the Quay, who looked a piratical and cutthroat gang and whose instructions were ignored by His Grace's crew, the *Sea Lion* was tied up alongside.

The Duke went below.

Breakfast was already laid for him in the Saloon and he seated himself with an expression of one who would be surprised if he found anything to tempt his appetite.

The stewards served him in respectful silence. They were too well trained to speak unless they were spoken to.

But gradually as he sampled the half-dozen dishes which had been prepared for him by a superlative Chef the Duke appeared to relax a little.

When breakfast was finished, still without a word uttered, the stewards withdrew and he sat alone in the luxurious Saloon of the yacht which had no equal in the world.

The *Sea Lion* had been delivered to His Grace only the previous year and last night when he had turned to leave the Casino he had remembered in the midst of his anger that she was in the harbour.

His carriage was waiting outside and as he stepped into it his Secretary and Comptroller of his house-hold,

Colonel Grayson, had come running down the steps of the Casino just before the coachman drove off.

"Are you leaving, Your Grace?" he had asked in a voice which held a note of incredulity in it.

"Yes!" the Duke replied in a monosyllable.

"Have you forgotten your supper-party? It is arranged as you requested."

"Cancel it!"

Colonel Grayson looked at him in surprise but merely murmured:

"I will do that, Your Grace!"

"Tell the coachman to take me to the yacht," the Duke said, "and what is more, Grayson, get all those people out of my Villa. With the exception of Mrs. Sherman, of course."

It seemed for a moment as if Colonel Grayson would protest and then he asked:

"Are they to leave at once, Your Grace?"

"First thing tomorrow morning," the Duke replied.

He spoke in a manner which told his Comptroller that he had no more to say on the matter.

Colonel Grayson stepped back and the footman wearing the Atherstone livery, which was as well known in England as that of the Royal Family, shut the carriage-door on which was emblazoned the Atherstone crest.

He obviously awaited instructions and Colonel Grayson with an effort said:

"His Grace desires you to take him to the yacht."

"Very good, Sir."

The footman sprang up onto the box, the coachman whipped up the horses, and they started off down the steep hill which led from the Casino to the harbour.

As the yacht put out to sea, nosing its way between the other ships moored in the small basin lying between the high rock on which was perched the Royal Palace and the white-domed Casino which looked like a wedding cake, the Duke stood on deck staring ahead.

He did not see the lights of Monte Carlo, which

gave it a fairy-like appearance, or the stars glittering overhead in the sable sky.

Instead he was concerned only with the darkness of his own anger which filled his mind to the exclusion of all else.

How could it be possible, he asked himself, that he should be in such an intolerable position and at the same time not have foreseen that he was running into disaster?

The Duke had been well aware ever since his boyhood that he was one of the greatest matrimonial catches in the whole of the British Isles.

The State in which his father lived was comparable only with that of a Royal personage, and while he was still in the Nursery he had known that it was all to be his one day.

The great broad acres of land which surrounded Atherstone Castle, the grouse-moors in Scotland, the hunting-lodge in Leicestershire, the ancestral ruins in Cornwall and the lands surrounding them, besides Atherstone House in London, would all be his.

And they were but a part of the incredible number of possessions, so many that it was impossible to remember them all.

Pictures, furniture, tapestries, treasures which had been handed down through the family for generations, besides a racing stud, carriage and hunting horses, and every other possession that a man could think of and desire.

Besides all this there were properties abroad, a house in Paris, a Château in the Ardennes where he could hunt wild boar, a Palazzo in Venice, and a Villa in Monte Carlo.

Was it possible to own so much and not be happy?

The fly in the ointment of course lay, he learnt as he grew older, in the number of women who wanted to own it with him.

By the time he left Eton there were already innumerable mothers contriving with every trick and lure to inveigle him into a position whereby he must become their son-in-law.

When the Duke was in a good mood he would

laugh at some of the tricks they employed to force from his lips the fatal invitation which would tie him to one woman for the rest of his life.

He had made up his mind that he would not marry until he himself positively wished to do so, and nothing would induce him to be captured like a lassoed steer in the manner that some of his friends had been.

The protocol of Victorian Society made it very difficult for an eligible bachelor to avoid the ambushes which were set for him.

To talk to any unmarried young lady alone for more than a few moments was paramount to offering her marriage. To dance with her twice was to set the gossips' tongues wagging, and a third time was the equivalent of an announcement in the Engagements column of the *Times*.

It was little wonder that men who wished to preserve their freedom avoided débutantes like the plague and fixed their affections on married women.

It was far less dangerous to risk the jealousy of a husband than the ambitions of an aspiring Mama.

Moreover, Society adjusted itself to making it easier for discreet liaisons between those of more mature years.

Following the example set by the gay Prince of Wales, *jeunesse dorée* found that beautiful young women after ten years of marriage, when they had presented their husbands with a son and heir, were only too willing to evoke the light of admiration in another man's eyes.

The Duke naturally had not refused an invitation when it was offered to him in the shape of provocative, sophisticated lips and questioning glances from under long, dark eye-lashes.

He had moved from one beautiful woman to another, or as one critic put it, "from *boudoir* to *boudoir*," until he had met Lady Millicent Wealdon.

"Millie," as she was known to everyone, even the adoring fans who bought post-cards of what were known as the "Professional Beauties," had excited him from the moment they met.

She was dark and willowy and with a full figure and tiny waist in the admired fashion of the moment.

The daughter of a Duke, she had been outrageous in many ways ever since she had left the School-Room. But then Lady Millie's beauty had made her sure that the world was there for her to walk on and accordingly she stamped on it!

Her parents, sensing that only to look at her was to be certain that there was trouble ahead, married her quickly when she was only seventeen to a man thirty years her senior.

Lord Wealdon was rich, important, *persona grata* at Court, and a crashing bore!

He was however proud of his wife's beauty and Lady Millie was clever enough to make him believe that all she enjoyed was the adoration of her admirers, *en masse,* and was not in the least interested in them individually.

There might have been some truth in this until the Duke came along.

The moment they looked at each other there had been a fire in their eyes that was unmistakable, and the passionate desire that drew them together was impossible to control.

The Duke had made love to many women but he had never found anyone so insatiable, demanding, or fiercely stimulating as Lady Millie.

It was impossible to conceal their infatuation for each other and the world knew about their liaison from the very moment of its inception.

As long as Lord Wealdon was prepared to turn a "blind eye" there were few who condemned their behaviour, although there were quite a number of smiles and sly innuendos.

Then unexpectedly Lord Wealdon died of a heart-attack.

Lady Millie was in deep mourning, Queen Victoria having set an example of heavy and prolonged gloom which every widow was expected to follow.

It had therefore been difficult for the Duke to see much of Lady Millie although there were a few snatched assignations during the first six months.

During the second period things became easier.

They had been invited to the same house-parties, and their Hostesses made quite certain that their rooms were not too far distant from each other.

Lady Millie could not yet attend full Court functions, race-meetings, or garden-parties, but she was staying in London at a home which was only a stone's throw from Atherstone House.

Their love-affair renewed itself with all the fire, excitement, and drama that had been theirs when they had first begun it.

And yet the Duke found himself chafing a little not only at the secrecy which must surround their meetings and which bored him, but also the fact that Lady Millie tried to tie him to her side.

He was used to roving freely as the spirit moved him from London to the country, from race-meeting to cricket-week, from Cowes, where he invariably won several races, to Epsom, where he had a number of horses in training.

Lady Millie began to pout when he left her and pout again when he returned.

He found it rather irritating.

Finally, when the prescribed year of mourning was almost at an end, she decided, without his having expressed the wish for her to do so, to join him in Monte Carlo.

The huge white Villa above the town with its fantastic and exotic tropical gardens had been built by his father.

It was large enough to house fifty guests.

There was really no reason why the Duke should not fill the Villa with his friends except that he had looked forward to a few weeks' quiet after what had been a strenuous Winter.

This was owing partly to his many sporting activities, but also because he was deeply concerned with the political situation. Although many of his friends did not realise it, he had great influence in the House of Lords.

"It will be fun to be in Monte Carlo again!" Lady Millie said firmly, "and we cannot go on playing this ridiculous game of hide-and-seek any longer! Besides, in a month's time I can put away my black gloves and know that I am a free woman!"

There was no mistaking what she meant by "free" and the look that she gave the Duke was an open invitation for him to declare himself.

And yet the words had not come to his lips.

He had supposed vaguely at the back of his mind that it was inevitable that he should marry Lady Millie, but somehow something prevented him from saying so.

His friends made it quite clear, in fact too clear, that they thought it was a foregone conclusion.

It irritated him when his name was linked with Lady Millie's obviously and then Hostesses said, with meaning behind the words:

"I have put you and dear Millie together—of course!"

He told himself that it was foolish to expect an element of surprise after the love-affair had gone on for so long.

Yet he felt that, because it was so obvious, some of the mystery and some of the thrill was lacking.

It had been there at first, but now they were moving along the path that all his other *affaires de coeur* had taken; a path that had grown familiar through the years by the tread of too many feet.

Millie would make him an acceptable wife.

Society preferred that there should be no surprises where their ranks were concerned and that members of one Aristocratic family should marry a member of another.

From this point of view Millie would be the right wife, the Duke thought. She would also look very beautiful in the Atherstone diamonds and would undoubtedly make him an excellent Hostess.

At the same time deep in his heart he knew that something was missing, although he was not certain what it was.

When Millie was in his arms, when her lips sought his greedily, he felt himself drowning in her sensuous, exotic fragrance which seemed to numb all criticism.

Then he could forget everything except the passion she aroused in him.

When they reached Monte Carlo he found he had an unexpected aversion to making love to her under the very noses of his other guests.

He could not explain his sudden revulsion even to himself.

It was just that he did not like the knowing look in his men-friends' eyes, the faint smile on the lips of the other women, the manner in which they took it for granted that he would spend the night in Millie's bed-room.

There was something in the way they said "good night," just as there was something in the way they said "good morning," which annoyed the Duke.

Also, something fastidious in himself rebelled against creeping along his own corridors after everyone was supposed to be asleep to enter Millie's bedroom surreptitiously and close the door quietly.

He knew that she would be waiting for him almost like a tigress in her lair, her arms reaching out to hold him captive and make him forget everything but her insatiable desire.

For the first two or three days after their arrival in Monte Carlo Lady Millie said nothing.

He knew that she looked at him with speculation which gradually became resentful, and he knew too what words were hovering on her lips.

But she was too astute and too experienced to reproach him directly.

At the same time there was an accusation in the very manner in which she spoke to him and the occasional sharp little note that crept into her voice.

The Duke could be very obstinate and very ruthless if he wished.

He told himself that he would not be coerced or bullied into doing anything he did not wish to do.

It was one thing for a women to attempt to excite his desire, another to demand it as if it were her right.

And yet he knew that Lady Millie thought that she had a right over him—a right that she expected would soon be expressed for all the world to recognise by an invitation to their wedding.

The sunshine was golden and warm at Monte Carlo, the garden was a dream of loveliness, the Casino filled with friends and acquaintances.

The Emperor and Empress of Austria, the Dowager Empress of Russia, the Kings of Sweden, Belgium, Serbia, and the Queen of Portugal were all staying at the Hôtel de Paris.

There were in the Casino an inordinate number of Russian Archdukes and Maharajas with the *demi-monde* of Paris dazzlingly bedecked with ospreys and incredible jewels.

The *Beau Monde* rubbed shoulders with them as they stood round the roulette tables and listened for the click of the white ball.

"Gaming is a great leveller," someone said to the Duke ironically.

But the evenings were an excitement of win or lose which never failed to enthral.

Then last night in the Casino the Duke had run into the Countess of Minthorpe, a *grande dame* of the old school and a close friend of Queen Victoria.

She was one of the few Hostesses in London who were important enough to declare openly their disapproval of the Marlborough House Set.

This was the fast and raffish collection of rich, gay, and beautiful people who circled round the Prince of Wales and his lovely Danish wife.

The Countess had however greeted the Duke most affably and he had responded with his usual courtesy until she said in her distinct, well-bred voice:

"I hear that you danced with my grand-daughter, Daphne, at the Marchioness of Salisbury's Ball last week."

With some difficulty the Duke remembered a rather nondescript and shy débutante to whom he had been introduced by his Hostess and had therefore been obliged to ask her to dance.

"You also had supper together, I believe," the Countess of Minthorpe continued.

Again after a distinct hesitation the Duke remembered that he had taken a married woman down to supper, but the girl with whom he had danced at the beginning of the evening had sat on his other side.

He could not recall now whether he had spoken to her but he was quite prepared to believe that she had been there.

"Yes, yes, of course!" he said. "She is just out this Season, I believe."

"That is right," the Countess of Minthorpe confirmed, "and I was telling His Royal Highness of your interest in Daphne. He very graciously intimated that both he and the Princess Alexandra would expect to be the first to be told the good news!"

The Countess of Minthorpe smiled, inclined her head graciously, and moved away to leave the Duke staring after her, bemused.

What she had intimated could not be true! Yet he knew that it was and that the Countess could make things very difficult for him.

He had forgotten that his friend the Marquis of Dorset had been pressured into marriage in just such a manner by an ambitious mother enlisting the co-operation of the Prince of Wales.

The Marquis had done no more than take the girl in question for a walk in the garden during a house-party.

"You are getting the girl talked about," His Royal Highness had been prompted to say. "You must behave like a gentleman and ask her to marry you."

Dorset had obliged, but the Duke of Atherstone told himself that he had no intention of being caught in the same manner.

At the same time it infuriated him.

He had been so careful not to get involved with any young woman or to give any match-making Mama the excuse of taking him to task.

Because he was upset, even though he did not show it, by his encounter with the Countess of Minthorpe he walked over to the roulette tables in search of Lady Millie.

She was standing watching the wheel spin, looking, he thought, extremely beautiful.

There was a spray of ospreys in her hair. She wore an emerald-green gown which was daringly décolleté, and the diamonds round her neck and in her ears echoed the sparkle in her eyes.

Someone had once told Lady Millie that she sparkled like champagne and she had not forgotten it.

She was always sparkling like a fairy on a Christmas tree and invariably the men who clustered round her laughed at her witticisms, at her remarks with their risqué innuendos, and the *double entendre* she could make of the most simple sentence.

To the Duke, feeling as if he had received a body-blow from the Countess of Minthorpe, she seemed safe and familiar, part of the world he understood—a world which was very far removed from the Social marriage-market in which débutantes were paraded like horses in an arena.

He joined a group of men talking to Lady Millie and they moved aside for him in a manner which showed that they thought he had a proprietary claim.

"Oh, there you are, Draco!" Lady Millie said as the Duke reached her. "I have been looking for you. Give me five thousand francs. I have lost all my money!"

The Duke drew a wallet from the breast-pocket of his evening suit.

He drew out the francs and gave them into Lady Millie's hand.

She took them from him slowly and without haste. Then she looked up into his face and said:

"At least—you are rich!"

There was no mistaking the meaning behind the words nor the look of frustrated resentment.

Just for a moment the Duke was still, and then he turned and walked away and out of the Casino.

He knew quite well that Millie was striking at him because she had waited for him the last four nights in vain.

She knew that in asking for the money in such a manner she was asserting her authority, showing the other people present that she had a claim on his wealth and could command it.

Perhaps if he had not already been incensed by the Countess of Minthorpe's words Lady Millie's taunt would not have inflamed him to the point when he knew that if he stayed in the Casino any longer he would lose his temper openly.

The Duke had always prided himself on his self-control.

He never raised his voice to a servant, he never quarrelled with anyone in words.

Instead, if he was annoyed he assumed an icy detachment, which was more effective than if he shouted or stormed at the person with whom he was incensed.

His voice could be like a whip-lash even though the words he actually used were not offensive.

Generations of pride and authority made him more awe-inspiring in his silence than anything he said.

At the moment he hated Lady Millie and the whole social structure which seemed to be encroaching on him, pressing him, harrassing him, forcing him into a corner to escape from which he would have to fight his way out!

He stood for a long time on deck until the ship was well out to sea and Monte Carlo looked like a fallen star in the distance, then he turned and went below.

Not to sleep, but to lie thinking of himself and a future which seemed unpleasantly full of hazards and obstacles.

Now coming into Algiers it was somehow a relief to think that he had put the whole width of the Mediterranean between himself and the Social world in which he lived.

He had been there before and it seemed to him that he needed the contact between the glittering, superficial, flamboyant Society playground of Europe and the Oriental mysticism of Algiers.

It was as if the Kasba called to him after the sophisticated luxury of the Casino.

He knew the narrow alleys so dark at times that a

pedestrian was compelled to feel his way, and in them
the men and women in their native costumes were buying, selling, eating, sleeping, praying, and gambling.

All in the tiny, confined spaces of their booths
where they sold jewels and silver, carpets and leather-
goods, and the more primitive requirements of an un-
civilised people.

He knew the smell there would be of heavy Arab
perfume thick with musk, of the strange dishes fried
in the open, of smoke from incense drifting through
the airless Bazaar, and the dry, acid scent of the desert
which seemed to come from the people themselves.

In his imagination it all seemed to welcome him
but he knew that before he explored the city he must
visit his friend—a friend of many years who was to him
an intrinsic and indivisible part of Algiers.

Although it was still early for calling the Duke
went from the Saloon to tell the stewards to hire him
a carriage and drove off from the Quay.

He journeyed not towards the Arab part of Algiers where once the blood-thirsty Barbary pirates
imprisoned thousands of Christian slaves working in
chair-gangs, but up through the modern French town
to where the white Villas were encircled like jewels
in a shrine of green.

There were palm, orange, plane, and pepper trees
everywhere and finally as he drove through them the
carriage turned up a short driveway to a modest-sized
Villa, white and simple, with an incredibly beautiful
view overlooking the bay.

The garden was full of blossom and seated on the
terrace where the Duke was shown by a servant were
a man and a woman.

For a moment they stared at him incredulously;
then the man jumped to his feet with an exclamation
of delight.

"Draco! Is it really you?"

"You are surprised to see me?" the Duke asked,
holding out his hand.

"Surprised? I am astonished!" Nicholas Vlastov replied. "Astonished and overjoyed."

The Duke's friend was a man little older than himself. Good-looking with that indescribably Russian charm which made him fascinating both to men and women alike.

He covered the Duke's hands with both of his, then with his arm round his shoulders he led him nearer to the table.

"Fatimat, my dear," he said, "here is our friend, Draco Atherstone, whom I could not be more delighted to see."

"I too am delighted to see you," Madame Vlastov replied.

Although the Duke had known Nicholas Vlastov for many years when he had been in the Diplomatic Service, he had only met Madame Vlastov once, and that was soon after they had run away together.

It had caused a great scandal at the time.

Nicholas Vlastov had been Russian Attaché at the Court of St. James, where he had gained a great deal of popularity and a considerable amount of respect.

He had returned to Russia on leave and inexplicably and without any warning left with the wife of a senior Diplomat whom he met in St. Petersburg for the first time.

They had fled to Algeria and it was five years before her husband finally agreed to divorce Fatimat and she was able to marry the man she loved.

They had been years of ostracism and persecution, years when nobody would speak to either of them, when they were denounced for their outrageous behaviour and they found it hard to live.

The Duke however had never lost touch with his friend and had in fact assisted him financially during the first years when at times it was difficult to know where their next meal was coming from.

Then Nicholas Vlastov had begun to write.

He sent his first book to the Duke, who had read it and taken it personally to a Publisher who was a friend.

He had expected to have to use his influence to get it published but the Publisher realised when he read Nicholas Vlastov's book that he was a hitherto undiscovered genius.

The first book was a huge success and a second and third which followed it were best-sellers not only in England but all over the world.

They were even translated into Russian, which was a personal triumph.

There was no doubt that Nicholas Vlastov was now a rich man, with every prospect of becoming very much richer.

But he would never forget those who had stood by him in trouble and there were very few of them.

As the Duke sat down at the breakfast table and accepted a cup of coffee he asked:

"Why are you here? Why did you not let us know you were coming?"

"It is a long story and not a particularly interesting one," the Duke replied. "Tell me about yourself. What are you writing?"

Before Nicholas Vlastov could answer he added another question:

"Are you both happy?"

Madame Vlastov put out her hand and laid it on the Duke's.

"We live in a special Paradise of our own," she said. "I wish I could describe to you how wonderful it is."

She was very beautiful in a Russian manner and the Duke raised her long, thin fingers to his lips before he said:

"Nicholas is a very lucky man. I am jealous of him!"

"I shall have to try and find you someone as alluring as Fatimat," Nicholas Vlastov said with a smile.

The Duke put up his hands in mock horror.

"No, no!" he said. "No more scheming, manoeuvring women! To be honest, that is why I am here!"

"I half guessed it," his friend said, "seeing that you have come alone."

He, perhaps better than anyone else, knew how the Duke was pursued, importuned, and harried by women.

They had spent some very gay and raffish times together both in London and in Paris.

Sometimes it had been only his Russian ingenuity which had extracted the Duke from almost impossible situations or imminent scandals.

"I want to be immersed in Africa," the Duke said. "What are the latest amusements to delight a bored and jaded man, to titillate the senses of someone who is satiated with the pleasures of European life?"

Nicholas Vlastov threw back his head and laughed.

"Draco, you will have to write a book," he said. "Such a flow of language would make you a best-seller the moment it appeared!"

"Like you!" the Duke answered. "Are the sheckels rolling in?"

"He is such a success!" Fatimat Vlastov said proudly in her soft, musical voice. "He is translated into almost every language in the world and his reviews are so flattering I am half afraid he will become conceited!"

"Not when I have a wife like you," Nicholas Vlastov said. "You are my severest critic. You always discover even the tiniest faults, so that I never get too puffed up with myself!"

She laughed at that but her eyes were full of love as she said:

"I may criticise, but you know as well as I do that I touch your feet in admiration."

For a moment it seemed to the Duke as if the two people on either side of him had forgotten his existence.

They were looking at each other with an understanding and a closeness which made everything else supremely unimportant.

'That is what I want,' he thought. 'That is what I am looking for in life.'

He had a sudden vision of Millie's beautiful face but with a very different expression in her eyes.

It was, he knew, the hunger of physical desire, the fire of passion, and also a greedy possessiveness —a struggle for power and supremacy, which was something he would never tolerate from a woman.

"What shall we do about you?" Nicholas Vlastov said. "Algiers, as you know, is full of all the curiosities and the sensations that the Arab world can devise."

"I have no desire for you to take me to the Dances of the Aissawa again," the Duke said. "Once was quite enough where they were concerned."

Nicholas Vlastov laughed.

His Slav blood had not been revolted by the fantastic religious dances which were often accompanied by the gouging out of eyes, the searings of hot irons, the piercing of cheeks with daggers, and the eating of live lizards.

The Duke however had said that the whole performance, while it had a weird fascination, had made him feel slightly sick.

"I can understand your not liking anything so horrible," Fatimat Vlastov said to the Duke, "but Nicholas tells me that such things are good copy and therefore I encourage him to go, so long as he does not tell me about them!"

"He is quite right!" the Duke said. "It is not the sort of spectacle for a woman to hear about, let alone see!"

Madame Vlastov rose to her feet.

"You can talk to the Duke of all those barbarian native customs which interest you," she said, "but I shall go into the house and think beautiful thoughts!"

"And look very beautiful while you do it!" her husband said. "You are quite right, my darling, it is not a subject which should concern you."

"I am glad we agree on that!" Madame Vlastov smiled and left them alone.

"She is very lovely!" the Duke said.

"I am the luckiest man in the world!" Nicholas Vlastov replied.

"You have never had any regrets?" the Duke enquired. "After all, you are very isolated here. Do you never miss the world outside? The cut and thrust of politics, the intrigues and excitements of diplomacy, the Society which still looks at you both with raised eyebrows?"

"I have always told you the truth, Draco," Nicholas Vlastov said. "I swear to you I did not know I could be so blissfully happy and I thank God every day on my knees that I was privileged to find the one person in the world who is the other part of myself."

He spread out his hands in an expressive gesture.

"We think the same, we breathe the same air, talk the same language. She is mine and I am hers. It is difficult to know where one of us ends and the other begins!"

"I am glad!" the Duke said.

"It is what I wish for you, Draco," Nicholas Vlastov said, "but I doubt if you would be happy away from the world you know. Your background, your sport, the brilliant chandeliers, the champagne, and the tinkling voices of beautiful women!"

"I wonder . . ." the Duke said reflectively, "but I cannot answer that question until I have found my Fatimat, which quite frankly I believe is impossible!"

"Perhaps you have too much already," Nicholas Vlastov said. "It is greedy to want more."

He smiled.

"And yet," he said, " 'to those who have shall be given.' You have an awful lot, Draco!"

The Duke did not answer and after a moment his friend said:

"Are you going to tell me what has upset you?"

"Not at the moment," the Duke answered, "perhaps later. I want to forget. I want to be amused. I do not want to have to think too seriously."

"Then as your host I must not fail you," Nicholas Vlastov said, "and tonight I will show you something you have never seen before and are likely never to see again."

"What is that?" the Duke asked.

He did not sound particularly excited and there was a somewhat cynical expression in his eyes, as if he felt there was nothing new he had not tried, nothing strange he had not seen.

"It will be hard but not impossible," Nicholas Vlastov said, "but I am going to arrange for us to be present at a Slave-Market!"

Chapter Two

"A Slave-Market?" the Duke exclaimed. "I thought they were abolished when the Barbary pirates were defeated."

"The pirates sold Christian slaves, the majority of them men," Nicholas Vlastov answered, "but Algerians never change. Today they sell women!"

The Duke raised his eye-brows and his friend went on:

"That again is not peculiar to this country, but in the Market to which I shall take you this evening the slaves are all European."

"I have heard of such things," the Duke said slowly, "but I did not believe them."

"You will be able to see for yourself," Nicholas Vlastov answered.

"And the buyers?" the Duke enquired.

"They are usually rich Sheiks who come to Algiers from the desert just for these Markets," Nicholas Vlastov explained. "They leave their wives at home and because they often find it difficult to take a new purchase back with them, the Bordels in Algiers have a new arrangement as regards these women."

"What is it?" the Duke enquired.

"After the auction the Sheik who buys one of the slaves leaves her in a Bordel, but she is his exclusive property as long as he wants her."

"He cannot take her away?" the Duke asked.

"No. Under the new arrangements that is impossible. Although she belongs to him so long as he is within the Bordel, the Patron who has brought her to Algiers really leases her out to the highest bidder."

The Duke said nothing and his friend went on:

"Usually, I believe, within six months the Sheik is looking round for a new girl to entertain him. His original purchase is then sold again for less money. When that arrangement finishes she becomes an ordinary inmate of the Bordel, earning money for the Patron."

Nicholas Vlastov made a gesture with his hands.

"You can guess the ending," he said. "When the girl loses her looks or when she becomes a helpless drug addict she is turned out into the streets."

"To die, I suppose?" the Duke remarked.

"Some of them may get jobs as cleaners in the Hotels. A few become beggars but none of them live very long."

"It is horrifying!" the Duke exclaimed.

"It is shocking in that the trade is gathering impetus and there is increasing demand for these white slaves."

"Are there many English among them?" the Duke asked.

"A few, I believe," Nicholas Vlastov replied. "The majority are Germans, particularly valuable because of their fair hair. Danish, Armenians, and Lebanese are also very popular."

"Are they kidnapped?" the Duke asked.

"At one time kidnapping in England reached quite frightening proportions," Nicholas Vlastov answered, "but now I am told there is a different approach. Usually the girls are enticed abroad by being offered what appears to be a good job."

"What as?" the Duke enquired.

"As Nursery maids, actresses, or simply chorus-girls. But more than anything else the *Souteneurs,* who are usually attractive and good-looking men, trick them with a promise of marriage. They even on occasion go through a marriage-ceremony which needless to say is only a farce!"

"Surely when they realise the truth the girls have some chance of escaping?" the Duke asked.

"If there were some chance the majority of them would not attempt it," Nicholas Vlastov replied.

"Why not?"

"Because they have already become drug addicts."

He paused before he continued:

"As you well know, Draco, it is very easy to obtain hashish in this country, also drugs like opium, heroin—the whole filthy list. Once a girl is 'hooked' she will never leave her source of supply."

"Surely something is being done about this?" the Duke asked.

"By whom?" Nicholas Vlastov replied. "I can assure you it is an extremely lucrative business and the Sheiks are prepared to pay considerable sums for their purchases. Those in the trade therefore become completely uncommunicative if questioned."

"I should be interested to see for myself what happens," the Duke said.

He thought as he spoke that his friend must be exaggerating.

He could not believe that the girls in question were anything but the dregs of the cities from which they came.

London, according to published statistics, was a hot-bed of vice.

The increase in prostitution had aroused the condemnation of the Church and there had been debates about it in the House of Commons and the House of Lords.

Two years previously the Criminal Law Amendment Act had been passed to make better provisions for the protection of women and children and for the suppression of brothels.

The Bill had been carried through by 179 votes to 71.

It was to be the first of the great battles against what was in effect slavery but the Duke knew that there must be many more before the Law could be effective in controlling what so many people thought was an inevitable condition in large cities.

The Duke spent the rest of the day in the Villa Shalimar with his friends.

There was so much to hear about Nicholas Vlastov's successes and his plans for the future.

After a delicious luncheon the two men went out into the garden while Madame Vlastov rested in the house.

Comfortable couches had been set in the shade of an acacia tree heavy with blossom.

There was the fragrance of flowers, the song of the birds, and below them the magnificent panorama of azure-blue sea stretching out towards the horizon.

Lying on his back and staring up into the green branches above him, the Duke felt rested and, for the first time since he had left Monte Carlo, at peace with the world.

He had forgotten, he thought, how much he missed Nicholas Vlastov, with his charm, his affection, and above all a kind of inner wisdom which the Duke had always relied upon.

He had found that he could talk intimately and seriously with Nicholas as he had never been able to do with any other man.

It was as if their friendship was so close it might have been one of blood, whereas in fact they had not met each other until the Duke went to Oxford.

He had been in his first year whilst Nicholas Vlastov was in his last, and yet instinctively they had gravitated towards each other and formed a bond which the Duke knew would never be broken.

"What are you writing now?" he asked, his voice rather slow and lazy, and yet it was not a casual question. He was really interested.

"I am writing a novel," Nicholas Vlastov answered, "but it is in fact the story of man's pilgrimage in search of himself!"

The Duke knew the mystic beliefs which lay behind all of his friend's writings and he asked:

"Is that what we are all seeking?"

"But of course," Nicholas Vlastov replied. "We all have a special 'Mecca' which we try to reach, but there are so many obstacles and indeed so many diversions on the way that it is not easy."

"And you think that you have found your 'Mecca'?"

"I have found Fatimat, which is the same thing!" Nicholas Vlastov replied. "You see, Draco, I have always believed that a man is not complete without the woman who is the other part of him."

"There have been many women in my life," the Duke said with a cynical twist to his lips.

"As I know," his friend answered, "but not one of them has been the one for whom you are looking."

"How do you know that?" the Duke enquired.

"Because what you are seeking, Draco, is quite simple. It is the other half of your soul."

The Duke was silent for a moment, partially in surprise, and Nicholas Vlastov went on:

"I try to show in my book that women are like flowers along the pilgrim's path we tread. Passion, unless there is something deeper behind it, dies as quickly as the flowers themselves."

"It can be very satisfying," the Duke said, thinking of Lady Millie.

"But of course," his friend agreed. "The physical union of a man and a woman is the expression of life —a reflection of the Divine Will for creation. But there is so much more to it than that."

"The meeting of souls!" the Duke said somewhat ironically. "Does it really exist, Nicholas?"

"Can you doubt that real love with a woman who is the other part of one's self is of God, while the imitation of which we have just been speaking is the work of the devil?"

He was silent for a moment and then he went on:

"But it can still be a step in a man's pilgrimage to discover himself."

The Duke thought over what his friend had said and after a moment he asked:

"And suppose a man never finds the woman who is the other half of his soul, as you put it—and may I say I consider it rather an over-emotional expression?"

"Then he must be prepared to accept the imitations, the substitutes, the second best," Nicholas Vlastov replied, "knowing all the time he is not satisfied and that something within him is well aware that he is being defrauded."

The Duke stirred restlessly.

"I think you expect too much!"

"Have not you and I always asked for the best in life?" Nicholas Vlastov enquired. "And when we were at Oxford we were determined to get it!"

"And you have not been disappointed?"

It was a question, not a statement.

"I have been blessed as few men are privileged to be," Nicholas Vlastov answered, "but I pride myself that I recognised what Fatimat could be to me the moment I saw her."

"Did it really happen like that?" the Duke asked.

"I walked into the Ball-Room of the Winter Palace and saw her among the splendour, the glitter, and the fantastic extravagance of the most lavish Court in the world. It seemed to me she shone with pure white light."

He paused before he went on:

"You will think I am exaggerating, Draco, but I am sure there was an aura round her which made me know that this was the woman I was seeking. She belonged to me."

"You were absolutely and immediately positive?" the Duke asked.

"More positive of that than of anything I have ever been in my whole life," Nicholas Vlastov answered. "I walked towards her seeing nobody and nothing but her face, and she told me that when she looked at me I was the man who had always been in her dreams."

"Why can that not happen to me?" the Duke asked.

Nicholas Vlastov smiled.

"You must believe," he answered, "and if you have faith, it will!"

"I doubt it!" the Duke said.

"What you will have to ask yourself is whether, when it happens—which I am convinced it will—you will be prepared to fight and battle for your fate."

"You certainly suffered for yours," the Duke said quietly.

"Not really," Nicholas Vlastov said. "I merely threw away a lot of old rags and put on an armour in which I was prepared not only to fight the world but to storm Heaven itself as long as I could have Fatimat."

"I envy you!" the Duke said. "Damn you, Nicholas, I envy you! Why can I not find a woman who will raise me to the heights of ecstasy which I can hear in your voice?"

"Perhaps you look in the wrong places," his friend replied dryly.

"I was thinking when I was coming here," the Duke said, "of the Slave-Market which exists in our so-called Society."

Nicholas Vlastov turned his head to look enquiringly at him, and he went on:

"What is it but a Slave-Market where débutantes are forced to marry the richest or most distinguished bidder and men like myself are pressured by every possible means, fair or foul, to bid for them?"

Nicholas Vlastov laughed.

"Poor Draco! Are they still trying to get you?"

"They are indeed!" the Duke answered.

He told his friend what had happened in the Casino and what the Countess of Minthorpe had said to him.

"You had better go round the world," the Russian advised. "It will take you away from the dangers that you have described so vividly and open up new horizons."

"I would go tomorrow," the Duke said, "if I thought it would not be a repetition of other visits."

Nicholas Vlastov laughed again.

"I know full well what they were like! Received in State by the British Ambassador, an audience with the King and Prime Minister, and the local beauties paraded for your inspection! Then, having given an excellent impression of the English Nobleman abroad, you passed on to the next port of call!"

The Duke laughed too, but rather wryly.

"Now tell me the rest of the story," Nicholas Vlastov suggested.

The Duke felt that he could not speak of Lady Millie, not even to his greatest friend.

The real reason, he told himself, was that he

could not make up his mind what he really felt for her.

She had been so much a part of his life during the last eighteen months that even after his anger last night he could not quite believe that the episode was finished.

He had come very near on a number of occasions to deciding that he must marry her. In fact he thought of it more often than he would admit to himself.

Now he felt that he was like a horse shying at an unexpected object in the road.

He wondered what Nicholas would think of her.

Would he believe that Millie was the other part of his soul?

Then he told himself that he did not know whether Millie had a soul. It was something which they had not discussed and indeed he would have felt embarrassed to do so.

He knew too, if he was honest, that he could not have the conversation he had just had with Nicholas with any woman of his acquaintance.

Women had always been there in his life to amuse and entertain; to make him laugh; to sweep away boredom and irritation; to prevent there being even the shadow of a frown between his eyes.

Millie had contrived to do this most successfully until the last four days.

He knew now that everything stemmed from the fact that he had not gone to her bed-room as she had expected; that he had not made love to her as she had demanded; and in consequence he was seeing a side of her that he had never seen before.

"No," he told himself now after some minutes' reflection, he was certain that Millie did not have a soul, but then doubtless he did not possess one either.

"Well, have you made up your mind not to marry her?" Nicholas Vlastov asked, breaking in on his thoughts.

"How did you know that that was what I was thinking?" the Duke enquired.

"It is obvious, is it not? The Countess of Min-thorpe, or whatever her name is, would not have upset you to the point of leaving the Casino at a moment's notice and arriving here at dawn looking disillusioned and cynical!"

"Is that how I appeared?" the Duke asked.

"I know you so well, Draco," Nicholas Vlastov replied. "You think you are tough and ruthless. In fact, although you would die rather than admit it, you are sensitive and at times romantic!"

"I deny it utterly!" the Duke said sharply.

His friend laughed.

"I knew you would. But, Draco, we have been too close for too long for me not to recognise the truth. You have been spoilt all your life by having too many possessions, but you are still a man who thinks. You have a brain, as well as an intuition which you seldom trouble to use."

"You sound like a fortune-teller in the Bazaar," the Duke remarked.

"And far more accurate than any of those charlatans could be," Nicholas Vlastov replied. "The reason I have always loved you, Draco, is that when I am speaking you understand."

He smiled as if to himself.

"Can you imagine that either of us could talk like this to any of those nitwits crowded round the tables in the Casino last night? How often I have seen them, the women with their claw-like hands, the men watching the ball with the concentration of a hawk!"

He threw out both his arms towards the tree above him.

"It is money, money, money they crave!" he cried, "and yet even that is better than emotional stagnation."

"Go on," the Duke prompted. "I am enjoying the rhetoric!"

"You know quite well what I am trying to say," Nicholas Vlastov answered. "Concentration, ambition, the striving for anything is an adventure. It is as exciting as galloping a wild horse across a plain, climbing a snow-peaked mountain, or fording a dangerous river!"

"You are telling me it is the effort which counts," the Duke remarked with a hint of amusement in his voice.

"Exactly, but the effort must be made. What comes from it is on the lap of the gods."

"I suspect that you are sending me off on a pilgrimage!" the Duke said.

"I am trying to do so! Forget what you have so far encountered on the way and go further," his friend begged. "Who knows what is waiting just over the horizon?"

"I would not mind betting," the Duke replied, "that there will be a profusion of those pretty and expendable flowers."

"But there is always another horizon beyond and again beyond," Nicholas Vlastov said quietly.

The carriage reached the entrance to the Kasba and Nicholas Vlastov told the coachman to stop.

The Souk, or market, clustered round the original Kasba which had been the Citadel and Palace of the Deys before the French conquered the city in 1830.

Under General Bourmont they had routed an Arab force of forty thousand men, and the piracy and slavery which had made the Mediterranean the most dangerous sea in the world came to an end.

Algiers had a very mixed native population ranging from Moors of mixed Spanish and Arab pedigrees to Bedouins and the Kabeles, who formed the largest part and were from the mountains.

They were a pure race showing traces of Greek and Roman elements in their complexions and their laws and having some of the Christian customs of the early centuries in their religion.

All these peoples with their colourful characteristic dress congregated in the Arab town around the Kasba.

Having left the carriage, the Duke and Nicholas Vlastov had to walk up narrow, steep streets forming an unbroken series of five hundred steps before reaching the eminence of the Dey's Palace.

Before they left the Villa Nicholas Vlastov had put an Arab head-dress on the Duke and a black cloak over his dark suit.

"Speak French," he said. "On no account let anyone know that you are English and therefore a foreigner!"

"What are you?" the Duke asked.

"I am a writer as well as a resident in the city. It is only in England where a 'man of letters' is not appreciated!"

The Duke laughed.

"I think that is true. The English have always suspected anyone who is too clever."

"Because of my success as a writer I have been allowed to see sights that no other outsider has seen, and I have been to places in the interior where a knife in the back is the reward of the curious!"

"I realise tonight I am privileged," the Duke smiled.

"You will be safe with me," Nicholas Vlastov replied, "but it is always wise to look like an Arab as one walks through the dark alleys. Once inside you will be accepted as my French friend and no questions will be asked."

They walked for some way, the Duke conscious that they were watched by many eyes even though he could not see to whom they belonged.

Most of the booths were closed but some were still open, lit by a flaming torch or a candle-lantern, and the coffee-sellers were still busy.

There was the atmosphere he had remembered as his yacht had entered the harbour.

The scent of sandalwood and ambergris, the smell of sand after the heat of the sun, and with it too the strange, mysterious aroma of North Africa, which was indescribable in words.

It was recognisable, just as all cities like Paris and London had their own particular, individual smell.

They had climbed almost to the top of the steps before Nicholas Vlastov stopped at the door of a tall, windowless house.

He knocked three times and after a short wait the door was opened.

He spoke to a servant in Arabic and they were invited in by the gesture of the man's hand. The door was closed and barred behind them.

They passed along several dark passages and through a court-yard where a small fountain tinkled musically into a stone basin.

A servant took the Duke's cloak and head-dress from him and they entered a room where about twenty middle-aged Arabs were lying on low divans which stretched round three walls of the room.

Many of them were smoking opium through hubble-bubble pipes and picking food off silver dishes which were placed on little brass tables.

Nicholas Vlastov and the Duke were shown to two adjacent divans nearest to the wall which was empty save for an expensive Persian rug on the floor.

The Duke expected that it would constitute a stage for the slaves.

The Sheiks did not speak to each other, apparently deep in contemplation of what lay ahead, and the Duke and Nicholas Vlastov were also silent.

There was one other new-comer after they had arrived, and then the room appeared to be full and there were no other divans unoccupied.

Onto the empty carpet walked a man whom the Duke imagined to be the Patron.

He spoke first in Arabic and then in French.

He explained that when he had invited his clients to attend here this evening he had anticipated that the girls they were about to see would have been in his care for some days.

However, since the ship in which they had been brought to Algiers had only arrived that afternoon they were in fact completely untrained and most of them unaware of where they were.

"That means they have been doped up to the time of their arrival!" Nicholas Vlastov whispered to the Duke.

"What does he mean by 'untrained'?" the Duke enquired.

"He means that he has not yet instructed them in the more erotic behaviour of what is now their profession."

The Patron was saying that he therefore craved the indulgence of his illustrious guests although he was certain that they would find it amusing to play teacher.

There was a faint murmur from the Sheiks at this and the Patron added some pungent details in Arabic which the Duke was glad were not translatable.

At a signal from the Patron the girls were led on-to the platform by a large Eunuch while another brought up the rear.

This the Duke guessed was not only to prevent them from escaping but to make sure that the purchasers did not handle the goods until they had paid for them.

As the Duke's divan was nearest to what constituted the platform, he could see the girls better than anyone else in the room.

They were, he realised, very young and each was wearing only one flimsy garment which did little to hide their nakedness.

It was made of gold-threaded gauze and slit up either side. It was in fact little more than a long, transparent apron back and front stretching from shoulder to ankle.

The girls stood still, as they had obviously been instructed to do, and the Duke realised that there were only ten of them while there were double as many prospective buyers in the audience.

This ensured, he thought, that there would be competition in the bidding, which was of course exactly what the Patron required.

There were three girls who he was certain were of German origin, with well-developed breasts and very fair hair. Although they were clearly of servant-class in Germany they were certainly attractive.

There were, the Duke guessed, one Dutch, two Danish or Swedish girls, two Armenians, and one Turkish, and one more whom he noticed last.

She was in fact the girl nearest to him but he

had not noticed her at first because her head was bent low on her chest and her long, fair hair had fallen forward to hide her face.

The Eunuch spoke to her sharply and the Duke saw her tremble as with what was obviously an effort she lifted up her chin to stare straight ahead.

It was then that he saw the terror in her eyes and realised, although he was not sure why he was so certain of it, that she was English.

She was much thinner and smaller-boned than the other girls and her tip-tilted breasts were small, or not fully developed. There was too a fawn-like grace about her which made her look very different from the heavily built, plump Germans at the other end of the line.

She had a heart-shaped face, a small, straight nose, and a perfectly shaped, sensitive mouth. The Duke was certain that she was of a class different from that of the other women.

Then he noticed that there was another very great difference that he had not perceived at first.

While the pupils of the eyes of the other nine girls were dilated and almost black with the drugs they had been given, the English girl was not drugged.

He was sure of it.

As she stood there he found himself speculating as to how she could have been brought to such a place.

She seemed very young.

The more he looked at her the more he was certain that she was well-born.

The German and Dutch girls were clearly low class, the Armenians and Lebanese had a slight flamboyance about them which made the Duke think that they had very likely been seeking employment on the stage before they had been approached or doped into coming to Algiers.

The Armenian girl had a dare-devil look about her while the Lebanese was obviously the foolish, rather giggly sort. She was, however, pretty in her way and full-chested, which was always attractive to Arabs.

His eyes went back to the English girl and as they

did so the Patron came out in front of them to explain that he would offer the girls one by one and the highest bidder would become her owner.

"Let me, however, remind you, Excellencies, that you cannot take the woman from the house. She will be yours just for as long as you want her. After that she will be resold."

The Sheiks grunted as if to say that they knew the rules and it was a waste of time having to listen to them again.

"Now shall we start the Auction?" The Patron asked.

There was an old man at the far end of the room who asked if he could first see the girls near-to.

"I like to know what I am buying!" he said in a harsh dialect.

The Patron gave permission for those who wished to approach the girls for whom they intended to bid. But he made it very clear that they must not touch them and it would be best if they did not enter into conversation with them.

The old Sheik who had asked permission to see the girls got to his feet and moved across the room.

The Duke saw that he had an eye disease very prevalent in Africa and he could understand why it was difficult for him to be sure of what he was buying at a distance.

He waited until there were more than half a dozen men on their feet looking the girls over as if they were animals, their dark eyes peering through the thin gauze with which the girls' bodies were inadequately covered.

Then he too rose to his feet, even though he sensed Nicholas Vlastov's surprise as he did so.

He had to take only two steps from his divan to reach the English girl.

He stood looking at her and she looked back at him with an expression that he had never before seen in a woman's eyes.

She seemed to shrink away; and then as if what she saw reassured her she whispered in English almost beneath her breath:

"Save . . . me! Save . . . me!"

Low though the whisper was, the Eunuch beside her heard it. He spoke sharply to her and his hand moved as if he would strike her.

The Duke contemplated stopping him by force. Then he turned on his heel to go back to the divan on which he had been lying.

"Be careful!" he heard Nicholas Vlastov murmur in French.

"I intend to buy her."

"If you do you will not be able to get her away from the building."

"I will still buy her. It will at least give us time to think how to rescue her."

"It is a crazy idea!" Nicholas Vlastov said sharply. "I did not bring you here for that."

"Look at her," the Duke said softly.

"I agree she is English and beautiful," Nicholas Vlastov answered, "but you cannot do anything about a woman who is once in their clutches. They will never let her go."

"Surely they will take more money for her?" the Duke suggested.

"I doubt it," Nicholas Vlastov replied. "They make their own rules, and anyway I have always had a suspicion that the man here is not his own master. There is, I am sure, a higher authority who owns these places."

He glanced at the Patron and went on:

"That man would not have the money himself to pay the *Souteneurs* to keep up the Bordel in such luxury and pay the cost of transporting the women from every part of Europe."

It made sense to the Duke.

At the same time he looked again at the English girl and knew, however crazy it might be, that he could not leave her here.

She was different, very different, in every way from the other women standing in line and she was, as his friend had said, beautiful.

But it was not the flashy, fleshy beauty of the other girls.

He had the impression as he looked at them that had they not been brought to Algiers they would still have taken up the oldest profession in the world.

This girl was different and yet, the Duke asked himself cynically, was he being very skillfully deceived?

It would be a clever act on the part of the Patron to have for sale one girl who was very different from all the rest.

Why was she not drugged as the others were?

There were many quesitons the Duke would have liked to ask but he was well aware that his friend was not joking when he warned him to be careful.

They were speaking in French but even so it would be easy for their attitude to arouse suspicion.

The Duke, having been to Algiers before, knew that anyone who looked suspicious ended up with a knife in his back, face down on some dung-heap.

He forced himself to sit back at his ease, sipping the champagne that had been set on a table in front of them together with a plate of small sweet-meats, mostly made with honey and nuts that were so beloved by the Moslems, whose religion did not permit them to drink alcohol.

Finally after a long inspection the Sheiks shuffled back to their divans and the bidding began.

One of the German girls was put up first.

Three of the Sheiks were interested in her. Finally she fell to one who held himself with a pride which came from ruling a tribe of some consequence.

She was taken away and the Sheik rose and followed her from the room.

After that one of the Armenians and a Danish girl were sold at very high prices.

The next German fetched a sum greater than what had been paid for the first.

The Patron looked round and the Duke had the idea that he was keeping the Lebanese and the Armenian girls to the end because he thought that they might arouse the most competition.

They had a flirtatious look about them and were

smiling and making eyes at the Sheiks who remained in the room.

The Patron beckoned with his finger to the English girl, who was not looking at him but staring straight ahead as if she could not bear to see what was happening.

The Duke could see a little pulse beating in her throat, which showed how frightened she was, and her hands were clenched so tightly that the knuckles showed white.

Because she did not obey the Patron the Eunuch gave her a push and she looked round desperately, like an animal cornered and unable to escape. Then she moved forward.

The Patron described her, as the Duke had supposed, as English, untouched, very young and very desirable.

There was something in the way he spoke that made the Duke feel that if he had a pistol at this moment he would not hesitate to fire it at the man.

The Patron asked for the first bid.

The Duke, too experienced at Auctions to rush in immediately, waited.

The sum offered by a Sheik who had so far taken no part in the Auction was not a large one and the Patron laughed at it.

Another offered twenty pounds more.

The original offer was then raised by the first man and for a short time the two men were duelling with each other, which made it quite clear to the Duke that they were not so much interested in the girl as in defeating each other.

Then unexpectedly he joined in.

He merely raised the last bid by ten pounds, thinking that it would be a mistake to draw too much attention to himself.

One of the previous adversaries capped it.

He put him up another ten pounds. This brought the sum to the amount equal to what had been offered for the other girls.

One of the Sheiks then fell out and fixed his eyes

on the Armenian girl and the other Sheik bid again, somewhat half-heartedly.

The Duke raised his bid by twenty pounds and there was no more opposition.

All smiles at having done so well, the Patron made a gesture to the Duke to follow the girl, who was being led from the room.

The Duke rose to his feet, then bent to speak to Nicholas Vlastov.

"If you go home send the carriage back for me," he said. "I may need it in a hurry!"

"For God's sake, Draco," his friend said, "do not take any risks. It is not worth it!"

"It was you who told me only this afternoon to fight for what I desired," the Duke answered with a smile.

Without waiting for an answer he went from the room.

Outside he was asked immediately for his money and he fortunately had enough on him to pay what was required.

It left him with only a few pounds, which he knew he would need for the inevitable drinks which would be brought to the bed-room.

He was not mistaken, for when he entered the room where the English girl stood waiting for him he was followed by a servant carrying a tray containing not only French brandy and Algerian wine but also a bottle of champagne and several sickly native liqueurs which were made from fruits.

The servant set the tray down on a low table, accepted the remaining notes that the Duke had in his wallet, and bowed his way from the room.

As he closed the door behind him the Duke looked at it to find, as he had expected, that there was no lock on the inside.

The girl was watching him, her hands clasped together, her face very pale, her eyes stark with fear.

The Duke turned round.

"Why have you . . . bought me? Why have I been sold?" she asked in a frightened voice. "I do not . . .

understand. . . . I do not . . . know what is . . . happening!"

"Try not to be frightened," the Duke said quietly. "I want to help you."

"Take me . . . away from here. . . . Please take . . . me . . . away," she pleaded.

"It is not as easy as that," the Duke answered.

As he spoke he walked across the room to the window.

It was heavily barred with elegant but strong ironwork, which made the room a prison.

There were no other exits except for the door through which they had come in and which opened onto the stairs where he had seen at least half a dozen Arab servants.

They were there for a purpose—he was well aware of that!

Beyond them there would be the court-yard and the dark passages before there was a chance of reaching the door onto the street.

While the Duke was wondering what to do he opened the bottle of champagne.

"What is your name?" he asked.

"Selina."

He poured a little of the champagne into two glasses.

He held out one to the girl.

She shook her head.

"It might be . . . drugged!"

"Is that how they have been trying to give it to you?" the Duke enquired.

"I have not dared to eat . . . anything for three or four days," she answered, "except for a little fresh fruit."

She saw that he was listening and went on:

"When I became . . . conscious in the ship I knew I had been . . . doped. It was something the man must have put in the coffee. After I had drunk it, I . . . remembered nothing . . . more."

There was a sincerity in her voice and the Duke knew that she spoke the truth.

"I am . . . frightened!" she went on after a moment. "Will you . . . call the police?"

"They would not help you," the Duke said quietly, "and for the moment I cannot think how I can help you escape."

"B-but I . . . have to! Do you not . . . understand? I have to!" she cried desperately.

She looked up into his face and said, with stark terror in her eyes:

"If you . . . cannot . . . help me . . . give me something with which to . . . kill myself. This . . . p-place is . . . evil. H-horrible!"

The Duke took a sip of the champagne he held in his hand.

"As I opened the bottle," he said, "I think you are safe in drinking a little. It will help you to be brave —as you have to be."

"I-if you cannot . . . take me . . . away . . . then I must . . . die! You . . . must . . . understand that."

The Duke looked round the room.

There was a low divan bed with a number of pillows and one sheet on it.

There was a low table on which reposed the champagne, two looking-glasses hanging on the wall, and a few primitive washing-utensils in one corner. Otherwise the room, which was small, was empty.

There was however a thick and expensive carpet on the floor and he knew that by Oriental standards it was luxurious.

He looked at the window again, then at the door, and an idea came to him.

He raised his head and stared up at the ceiling, remembering that native houses had flat roofs, where in the heat of Summer the inhabitants invariably slept.

There would, of course, be a proper stairway to the roof somewhere in the house, but there was a chance—a slender one, but nevertheless a chance— that some of the bed-rooms would have trap-doors which could be opened to let in air when the rooms became completely stifling.

The ceiling had recently been painted but after a

long scrutiny the Duke discerned what appeared to be the outline of a small square just above the bed.

He crossed the room to the table on which reposed the washing-utensils. He place the ewer and basin on the floor and lifted the table up in his arms.

He kicked aside the bed and set down the table very quietly for fear that anyone listening would hear him moving the furniture about.

"Talk to me!" he ordered the frightened girl. "Talk in English and say anything you like, but try not to sound afraid. People will be listening. They will want to hear that you are entertaining me."

"They . . . said," she answered in a whisper, "that if we . . . did not . . . do as we were . . . told we would be . . . beaten. They . . . beat one girl on the . . . ship. It was . . . horrible!"

He saw a shudder go through her and said sharply, because he knew that it would make her pull herself together:

"Do as I tell you! You will have to help me, otherwise I shall have to leave you here!"

He saw Selina's eyes open wide with the terror that his words inspired.

Then with what he thought was commendable intelligence she began to recite a poem:

> "In the desert a fountain is springing,
>   In the wide wastes there is still a tree."

The Duke recognised Byron's lovely stanzas to "Augusta."

> "And a bird in the solitude singing
>   Which speaks to my spirit of thee."

Despite her fear the Duke realised that Selina's voice was musical and very cultured.

> "Alas! they were so young, so beautiful
>   So lonely, loving, helpless."

'Byron might have been writing of her,' he thought.

All the time she was reciting he was arranging the table, then climbing onto it to push with all his might at what he thought must be a trap-door in the ceiling.

At first it appeared to be stuck with the fresh paint and, perhaps because it had not been used since the previous Summer, it resisted his endeavours.

The Duke was very strong.

He rode every day when he was in England, boxed regularly with a professional pugilist in the gymnasium at his Castle when the weather was too bad to take out the horses.

This kept him amazingly fit despite the dissipation in which he frequently indulged.

"Too many and too big rich meals!" one of his instructors had said to him, "and far too much good wine!"

The Duke had laughed.

"Would you take away from me all the pleasures in life?" he asked.

"I would have you as you were meant to be, Your Grace," the instructor replied, "a young Samson!"

The Duke had laughed again but he had been flattered.

Now as he felt the trap-door begin to move under the pressure of his hands he thought that he had never been so glad that he was strong.

It took in fact a considerable effort to get it open, and as finally it fell back onto the roof the Duke realised that it had not only been stuck with paint but he had broken the hinge of the bolt with which it had been fastened down.

Now that he had succeeded in effecting an exit there was no time to lose.

He looked down at Selina, who was watching him and still reciting:

"But tell of days in goodness spent
A mind at peace with all the world,
A heart where love is innocent!"

"Give me that sheet," he said quietly.

She looked, surprised, but she obeyed him.

He pushed it out onto the roof above his head and looking up saw the stars bright in the sky, the brilliant, large, glittering stars of Africa that seemed to hang like lamps in the velvet darkness.

Then he stretched down and without asking questions Selina put her hand in his.

He pulled her up onto the table and, lifting her up in his arms, pushed her through the opening above him.

She was very light and it took her only a second to scramble onto the roof.

The Duke then raised himself on his arms, glad that his long sessions on the parallel bars enabled him to do so without difficulty.

What was difficult, however, was to squeeze himself through the opening of the trap-door. His shoulders were broad and the hole had been designed to let in air, not a large Englishman.

The Duke clambered out onto the flat roof.

There were plants growing in pots set along the edge of it and he saw that in fact it was not very big.

Very softly he put the trap-door back into place and said:

"Now we have to be clever! Pray Heaven you have a head for heights!"

By the light from the stars he saw two very large eyes looking at him and knew that Selina was no longer as terrified as she had been before.

There was a look of trust on her face.

The Duke bent and picked up the sheet.

"Come on!" he whispered urgently, "and move quickly!"

Chapter Three

The Duke took Selina by the hand and went to the edge of the roof.

As he had expected, the roofs in the Souk either touched each other or were so near that it was easy to leap from one to another.

Fortunately it was early in the year and he could not see anyone sleeping out, as they would when the weather was hot.

He turned to the side where the houses were built on the down-slope of the hills and stepped past the pot-plants and over the parapet onto the next house-top; then hurrying across the flat surface, he pulled Selina onto the next.

As they continued down the hill they found that each roof was lower than the one before it and usually the Duke had to step, climb down, and then lift Selina after him.

He knew as he held her almost naked body that she was trembling, but she did not speak and she ran as swiftly as he did despite the fact that she was bare-footed.

At last when they had travelled quite a way from the Bordel they found that they were looking into a narrow alley which ran diagonally between them and the next house.

It was a long drop to the street, with every chance, the Duke thought, that one of them might break a leg in falling.

He went to the other side, where he could see below there was a small, square roof jutting outwards.

It was a depth of about ten feet but without speaking the Duke let himself down by his hands from the parapet of the house on which they were standing and it was firm beneath his feet.

He reached up for Selina and she let herself down by her hands and he held her first by her legs, then her waist, and she was beside him.

The next drop, he saw, would land them in a small court-yard.

It had a door which led into the street and he could only hope that it would not be locked.

As they had done before, they let themselves drop into the court-yard.

Everything seemed to be quiet and the Duke saw that it was a dirty, unkempt place stacked with boxes and bales, obviously the back of a shop. There was a chance that the house-holder did not sleep on the premises.

The Duke walked very quietly across the rough stones of the court-yard and turned the handle of the door.

To his consternation it did not move.

He tried again but it was firm. Then Selina touched his shoulder and when he turned to look at her he realised that she was pointing with her finger high above his head.

The door was bolted.

The bolt was stiff but he drew it back and then found that there was another bolt at the bottom of the door.

He pulled it open and they slipped outside.

They were in a small *cul-de-sac* and just below them was the narrow alley-way they had seen from the roof.

While they had been moving swiftly across the roofs the Duke had wound the sheet he had brought from the bed-room of the Bordel into a loose rope and tied it round his waist.

How he took it off and put it over Selina, covering her head and seeing with satisfaction that it reached down to her ankles.

"Now you look like an Arab woman," he said. "Keep it close against your face."

She did not answer but pulled the sheet round her as they moved towards the alley-way.

"We will walk swiftly but we will not run," the Duke said, "as that would arouse suspicion."

He spoke very, very quietly, feeling as he did so that there were always ears to listen and eyes to see in a native quarter.

The alley-way seemed deserted and there were only windowless houses and a few cats and dogs lurking round the débris which had been put outside the closed doors.

They moved quickly in what the Duke felt must be the direction of the main entrance to the Kasba.

He did not dare attempt to find another exit. Suddenly they could hear behind them the sound of someone approaching, heavy foot-steps ringing out in the silence of the night.

They were coming nearer and Selina looked over her shoulder nervously.

"We must run!" she whispered.

The Duke without replying took her by the arm and drew her almost roughly into the doorway of a house.

There was only the protection of a few inches where the door was set back slightly from the road.

But he stood in front of her and knew that with his dark suit the man who was approaching them would not notice them until he was at least level.

The foot-steps came nearer and nearer, and when the man was within a few feet of where they were hidden the Duke was able to see that it was one of the large, heavily built servants he had seen in the Bordel.

There was no mistaking the clothes he wore and in the light from the stars the Duke could see that he carried in his hand a knife.

Without waiting to think, without hesitating, the Duke sprang from his hiding-place and struck the man a blow on the side of his face.

The Arab, taken by surprise, staggered and as he did so instinctively raised his knife.

With the skill of an experienced pugilist the Duke struck the man's hand upwards with his left fist and punched him hard with his right, this time on the point of the chin.

The man fell backwards and as he did so the Duke hit him again and again.

The knife clattered from his hand to the ground and he fell, hitting his head as he did so against the edge of a door-step.

The Duke stood over the man; his fists were still clenched but he no longer moved.

Without wasting any more time the Duke reached out again for Selina and, taking her hand, hurried her down the alley-way.

Now they were both running and had gone only a short distance when the Duke with a sense of utter relief saw ahead of them the steps up which he and Nicholas Vlastov had climbed.

He knew that below, waiting for them at the entrance, would be the carriage.

They turned downards but not before the Duke had seen coming down the steps towards them but still some distance away another servant dressed in the same manner as the one he had struck.

As he and Selina ran the man began to shout at them.

They were words which they could not understand. At the same time his voice echoed eerily and menacingly out of the darkness.

They reached the entrance. For a moment the Duke thought that the carriage was not there and then he saw it a little way down the road.

He reached it, pulled open the carriage-door, and almost threw Selina inside.

"To the Quay!" he said to the coachman, and as the man whipped up the horses they were away.

They were both panting with the speed at which they had run and Selina's breath came almost sobbing-ly from between her parted lips.

"We have done it!" the Duke said in a tone of triumph.

He could hardly believe even now that he had been involved in such a crazy and what he knew was a fool-hardy adventure.

If the first servant had not been taken by surprise there was every likelihood that at this moment he

would have been lying dead or dangerously wounded
in the gutter while Selina would have been taken back
to the Bordel.

.   There would be no redress.

Even if he had survived and tried to bring charges
against his assailant there would have been dozens
of witnesses paid to say that he was drunk, had
deliberately started a fight, and that the man in question was nowhere near him at the time of the at-
tack.

Foreigners who walked in the Souk at night de-
served what was coming to them.

But the Duke thought with a sense of elation that
he had succeeded although the odds must have been
against him doing so.

"Where are . . . you taking . . . me?" Selina asked
at length, although it was obviously difficult for her
to speak.

"Back to England eventually," the Duke replied,
"but the first thing is to get away from Algiers."

He was certain that he would be a target for
vengeance if he remained in the vicinity.

He only hoped that Nicholas would not suffer for
what after all was his crime, but he was sure that his
friend was too respected and too well known to the
authorities and people of importance for anyone to at-
tack him.

He might find it difficult to attend another Slave-
Market but that would doubtless be of little consequence.

The carriage drew up at the Quay and the Duke
leant out of the window to direct the man to go as near
as possible to the *Sea-Lion,* which was still some distance away.

When they were within a short walking distance
the Duke got out and said to the coachman:

"Tell your master I am deeply grateful to him. Say
that you have brought me here to my yacht and he
will understand it is important that I should leave
Algiers."

The man nodded and appeared to understand.

Looking about and seeing few people in sight except fishermen concerned only with their boats, the Duke drew Selina from the carriage.

She had pulled the sheet tightly round her and he put his hand under her arm and led her the short distance to the *Sea Lion*.

There were two sailors on duty as he stepped aboard and the Duke said urgently:

"Tell Captain Barnett to put to sea with all possible speed!"

"Aye, aye, Your Grace."

The Duke led Selina down the companion-way.

The design and furnishing of all the cabins in the *Sea Lion* had aroused admiration when she was first launched, and graphic descriptions of them had appeared in the *Illustrated London News* and the *Sporting and Dramatic*.

She had two master cabins larger than the others and even more luxurious.

The Duke occupied one and he took Selina into the other.

As he did so the steward who valeted him appeared in the passage-way.

"Give me one of my night-shirts," the Duke commanded.

The man fetched one from the next cabin.

It was of pure Chinese silk and specially made for the Duke at one of the most expensive outfitters in St. James's.

He took it from the valet and handed it to Selina, who was standing in the centre of the cabin clutching the sheet round her and looking bewildered.

"What I suggest," the Duke said quietly, "is that you put this on and get into bed. I am going to order you some food, and then when you have eaten it you must go to sleep."

"I am . . . safe?" she asked, and she sounded like a child who needed reassuring.

"You are completely safe!" the Duke replied. "In a very few minutes you will feel the yacht begin to move out of the harbour and tomorrow we will make plans for your future, but not now. We have both been through quite enough for one night!"

As he spoke he smiled at her the beguiling smile that women invariably found irresistible.

He could see her eyes looking at him apprehensively and knew that she must still be trembling as he had felt when he had lifted her down from the roofs of the houses.

He went from the cabin, closing the door behind him.

Outside he said to his valet:

"Get the lady an omelette and some soup—anything that the Chef can prepare quickly, and take her a glass of wine, although I dare say she would prefer tea. She is English!"

He felt that the valet, having seen the sheet Selina had been wearing when she came aboard, would expect her to be an Arab.

The man's face however was quite expressionless as he said:

"Very good, Your Grace, and what about you?"

"I will have a glass of brandy," the Duke answered. "I think I have earned it!"

"I'll bring Your Grace another coat," the valet said.

The Duke looked down and realised for the first time that his coat was not only dirty from where it had rubbed against the walls as he had let himself down from the roof-tops but both sleeves were torn at the seams.

The Duke smiled to himself.

The close-fitting, smartly cut suit, made in Savile Row, had not been intended either for the gymnastics he had undertaken in it or for his pugilistic efforts.

He looked at his knuckles and realised that they were bleeding slightly from the force with which he had hit the servant.

He thought with satisfaction that he had taught the man, if he survived, a lesson he was not likely to forget.

As he walked into the Saloon and poured himself a glass of brandy from a crystal glass decanter he thought how shocked and surprised the majority of his friends would be by what he had done tonight.

They were used to seeing him in the Jockey Club Stand at race-meetings, in the Royal Enclosure at Ascot, White's Club in St. James's Street, and an honoured guest in the most exclusive mansions in London.

They would never believe that he would stoop to embroil himself in what to them would seem an unsavoury intrigue in an Arab city.

The valet returned to the Saloon, carrying the Duke's smoking-jacket of claret-coloured velvet frogged with black braid.

The Duke put down his glass and allowed himself to be assisted out of his torn and dirty coat and into the smoking-jacket.

"I have ordered the food, Your Grace."

"Let me know when the lady has finished and you have taken the tray from her cabin," the Duke said.

"Very good, Your Grace."

The Duke thought it would be best to have a word with Selina before she went to sleep and reassure her that she need no longer be afraid.

He had the feeling that she was still so bewildered that it would take a long time for her to appreciate that her fears need no longer exist.

'I will send her back to England as soon as she is strong enough to travel,' the Duke thought. 'Her family must be frantic at her disappearance. Men who are instrumental in kidnapping or seducing innocent girls should be strung up and hanged.'

He decided that he would speak more forcefully in the House of Lords than he had done in the past.

He was quite certain that there would soon be more Bills on prostitution coming before Parliament and he decided that one of the first things he would do on his return to England was to look into the subject personally.

"The whole thing is disgraceful and unspeakable!" he told himself. "It must not be allowed to continue, at any rate in England!"

There was a knock on the Saloon-door and the Captain entered.

"Forgive me for disturbing you, Your Grace,"

Captain Barnett said, "but I was wondering where you wish to go."

The Duke was about to reply "Monte Carlo" when he realised that Selina had no clothes and despite his instructions Colonel Grayson might not yet have emptied the Villa of his guests.

There was every likelihood that however tactfully and diplomatically Colonel Grayson might approach them they would refuse to hurry their departure.

His friends the Fitzgeralds, who were staying with him, had a large number of acquaintances in Monte Carlo and he was certain that they would soon find themselves accommodation at another Villa.

The same applied to the Kenningtons.

Members of the smart, gay Marlborough House Set were welcome guests in every playground of Europe.

That left, he thought, Lady Millie!

Would she leave?

He had the uncomfortable feeling that she would be very difficult about it.

He realised that the Captain was waiting and after a moment he said:

"The Balearic Islands, Captain Barnett. We can anchor in Ibiza for the night and tomorrow I will make a further decision."

"Very good, Your Grace."

Captain Barnett left the Saloon.

He was a man who, the Duke knew, never asked unnecessary questions and never appeared surprised at whatever orders he was given.

The Duke drank a little more brandy.

Now his brain, with its well-known attention to detail, was working out a plan.

There would be clothes of some sort which his valet could buy for Selina in Ibiza.

He would talk to her, find out her parents' name and address in England and send them a telegram.

When they returned to Monte Carlo he would fit her out for the journey and send her home, if possible in the care of some sensible woman traveller.

She would be too frightened, he thought, to undertake such a long journey alone after all she had been through.

He confessed to feeling extremely curious as to how she had been captured in the first place.

To know this would be a help in the investigations he was determined to make.

He was still thinking over what lay ahead when his valet opened the door.

"The young lady has finished her supper, Your Grace. She couldn't eat much, but she asked me to thank the Chef and Your Grace for your kindness in thinking of it."

"First thing tomorrow morning, Gregson," the Duke said, "I want you to go ashore and buy the young lady some clothes, at any rate enough until we return to Monte Carlo."

"In Ibiza, Your Grace?" Gregson asked.

"I am not expecting you to be able to find Parisian creations," the Duke said, "but something which will cover her until we have a chance to buy something better."

He paused and then as if he felt an explanation was necessary he said:

"The young lady had been kidnapped. I therefore have had to help her escape at a moment's notice without her being able to bring anything with her."

"For a ransom, I suppose, Your Grace?" Gregson remarked. "It's just the sort of thing them thieving, cheating riff-raff would do! I never did trust any of them any further than I could throw them!"

The Duke did not contradict the valet's assumption that Selina had been kidnapped for money.

He had no desire for his crew to know precisely in what circumstances he had found her.

They had enough to talk about as it was.

"Well, do your best, Gregson," the Duke said, "otherwise the young lady will not be able to leave her cabin."

"I'm not very optimistic about what I'll find, Your Grace," Gregson replied.

The Duke finished his brandy and rose to his feet.

He walked along the passage-way, knocked on the door of Selina's cabin, and entered.

The light by the bed-side had not been extinguished and he could see her head on the pillow, her fair hair falling over her shoulders, pale gold as the first fingers of the sun.

Her eyes were closed and he realised that she was asleep.

It was a sleep, the Duke thought, of complete and utter exhaustion.

One of her hands lay on the outside of the bed-clothes and her fingers were open. Somehow it made her seem utterly defenceless.

'She is very young,' the Duke thought, looking down at her.

At the same time, now that he saw her face in repose and without the expression of fear, there was no doubt that she was very beautiful.

However, it was not the sort of beauty he would have expected to appeal to the Sheiks and Arabs, who liked their women plump and heavy-bosomed and believed that a thin wife implied a niggardly and mean husband.

He was not even certain that her beauty would be appreciated by the Socialites who had become used to the acclaimed loveliness of the majestic Lady de Grey or the tall, imperious figure of the Duchess of Sutherland.

Lilly Langtry had captured the affection of the Prince of Wales and the imagination of the public.

She too had a presence and carried herself like a Queen.

'This child is different!' the Duke thought to himself, and yet he could see that there was something as lovely about her as the poems she had recited so desperately at his command while he had opened the trap-door in the roof.

She must be intelligent, he thought, to have done exactly as he had told her and she must also have been well educated.

"I will get her back to her parents as soon as pos-

sible," the Duke told himself. "Then she will be able
to forget this unfortunate occurrence."

He bent forward to put out the light at the side of
the bed and went quietly from the cabin, closing the
door behind him.

When the Duke awoke it was to find that the
yacht was in harbour and the engines were still.

He had slept, he found, longer than he had expected.

As he stirred he realised that the evening had
taken its toll of his strength, strong though he was.

His right arm still ached at the pressure he had had
to exert to get the trap-door open and his knuckles
were not yet healed.

Nevertheless he had given a good account of himself.

He looked forward to relating to his instructor in
the art of boxing exactly how he had avoided the
thrust of the knife and caught the man on the point of
the chin.

He felt hungry and rang for his valet.

His call was answered by another steward.

"I beg your pardon, Your Grace," the man said,
"but Gregson has gone ashore, he said on Your
Grace's instructions."

"Yes, of course," the Duke answered.

The steward who had assisted Gregson on various
occasions shaved the Duke with an experienced hand
and brought him the clothes he required.

"Has the young lady rung yet?" the Duke enquired.

"No, Your Grace, and I thought it wise not to
disturb her until she did."

"Quite right!" the Duke approved. "Let her
sleep."

He went into the Saloon and ate a large breakfast.

He had just finished when Gregson appeared with
some parcels under his arm.

"Well, Gregson?" the Duke asked.

"I've never seen such an outlandish place, Your
Grace. You'd think the inhabitants wore nothing but

wode for all they can buy for themselves in the few
shops there are."

"You managed however to get something?" the
Duke enquired.

"I don't know whether Your Grace will approve,"
Gregson answered, "but I persuaded the young lady in
the shop to sell me a dress she had made for the
Festival next month."

As he spoke Gregson put down the parcels and
opened one.

He drew out what the Duke recognised as a typical
Spanish peasant's dress with full skirt, laced black
bodice, white blouse with low neck and short sleeves.

"There was nothing else, Your Grace," Gregson
said with a note of anxiety in his voice, as if afraid
that the Duke would be annoyed.

"I think you have done very well, Gregson," the
Duke answered. "At least it will be becoming!"

"There are petticoats and an apron, Your Grace.
I had to pay more than they are worth but it was this
or nothing."

"I am sure no-one could have done better!" the
Duke said and he was smiling as he left the Saloon.

It was some time later before, seated on deck
away from the wind in a place he usually found con-
venient for reading, he heard a light foot-step.

He looked up and saw Selina.

She was wearing the peasant-costume that Gregson had bought and she had plaited her hair and tied
the plaits round her head with a ribbon.

The Duke, rising to his feet, thought that her eyes
were even larger than he had at first remembered.

Now in the daylight he saw that they were very
deep blue, almost the colour of the sea during a storm.

"Good morning!" she said in a rather breathless
little voice which he thought still held a touch of fear.

"Come and sit down, Selina," the Duke said, in-
dicating a chair next to his own, "and may I say how
becoming that costume is to you?"

Selina put her hand up rather nervously to the low
neck.

"Your valet explained it was the only thing he

could buy me. I feel I look rather strange in it, but I am very grateful!"

"When we get to Monte Carlo," the Duke said, "I will buy you some proper clothes in which you can travel back to England."

Selina hesitated for a moment and then she said:

"I think I ought to tell you . . . at once that I have no . . . money and it will be a . . . long time before I can give you . . . back what you paid for me last . . . night."

"There is no need for you to do that."

"But I must! Of course I must!" Selina insisted. "The only difficulty is that I am not . . . certain how it can be . . . done."

"Suppose we start at the beginning," the Duke suggested. "I know your name is Selina, but last night we had very little time to introduce ourselves."

"I know that," Selina said apprehensively. "But before I spoke of anything else I should have . . . thanked you. I am so grateful . . . so deeply, over-whelmingly . . . grateful that I just cannot find . . . words in which to . . . express myself."

There was a little throb in her voice, as if she was not far from tears, and the Duke said quickly:

"I do not want your gratitude."

"Why did you . . . do it?" Selina asked.

The Duke hesitated for a moment before he answered:

"Shall we say that because I am English I could not allow a fellow-countrywoman to be treated in such a manner?"

He smiled.

"We were both lucky—very lucky—to get away as we did."

"It was only because you were so . . . clever and so . . . brave," Selina said, "and you . . . knocked that man . . . down in the . . . alley . . ."

"Forget it!" the Duke interrupted. "Forget everything that happened last night! All I want you to tell me is who you are and how you ever allowed yourself to be trapped into such a dreadful situation."

She did not speak and after a moment he said:

"I am sure also that you will want me to let your family know that you are safe. They must be very worried about you."

"I have no family."

The Duke raised his eye-brows.

"I cannot believe that anyone is completely without relatives."

"It is true where I am concerned," Selina answered.

The Duke looked surprised and then after a moment he said:

"Suppose you start by telling me your name."

"It is Selina Gretton."

"And your father and mother are dead?"

"Mama died two years ago. It was a very cold winter, if you remember, and she got pneumonia. The Doctor said that if we had been rich enough to send her to a warmer climate she might have . . . survived."

There was a pain in the musical voice which was inescapable.

After a moment the Duke said gently:

"And your father?"

"Papa died two weeks ago at least—but it may be longer. I lost all sense of time when I was on board the ship."

"Where did you live?" the Duke asked.

"We lived in the country in a tiny village called Coombe-on-Avon in Worcestershire. Papa and Mama went there to live when they ran away together!"

"Tell me about it," the Duke prompted.

"Papa was a musician. He played both the piano and the violin and when he was young he gave concerts. Some of the critics spoke very glowingly of him."

"What happened?" the Duke asked.

"He had a carriage accident and injured the little finger of his left hand. It meant that as a performer his career was finished and so he took to writing music."

Selina looked away from the Duke across at the blue sea, the waves glinting in the sunshine.

"Some of his music was beautiful! Very beautiful!"

"Why did he have to run away with your mother?"

"Soon after his accident, when he had to make money, as he could no longer give concerts he took up teaching."

"And one of his pupils was your mother?" the Duke interposed, conjecturing already how the story was going to evolve.

"How did you guess?" Selina asked. "They fell in love with each other, and naturally my Mama's father was incensed at the idea."

"A penniless suitor!" the Duke said with a smile.

The story, he thought, had the plot of a popular romance.

He could not help wondering whether Selina was telling the truth and yet it was impossible to doubt the honesty in her eyes or the sincerity in her voice.

"Papa was turned out of the house and forbidden ever to see Mama again," she went on. "By that time Mama knew that she could not live without him. She climbed out of her bed-room window one night and ran away with little more than the clothes she stood up in."

"It seems to be a habit in your family to travel light!" the Duke said with a smile.

"No-one could have worn . . . less than I did . . . last night," Selina said.

He saw the colour come flooding into her cheeks and her eyes dropped before his.

'No-one could act as well as that!' he thought to himself. 'She is speaking the truth, I am sure of it!'

"At first Papa and Mama nearly starved," Selina went on, "but then Papa sold a song he had written. He did not really like writing songs."

"But he very sensibly decided it was best to make money," the Duke said.

"He never made very much," Selina answered, "but we managed to be very happy!"

"Your father went on composing?" the Duke asked, wondering if he had ever heard of a composer named Gretton.

"He changed his name to Franz Lischen," Selina explained. "His grand-mother was Austrian and so he used her name, hoping that if people thought he was a foreigner they would be more interested in his compositions than if he was English."

The Duke remembered what Nicholas Vlastov had said about a man of letters not being appreciated in England and thought that the same would apply to composers and writers in every category.

"Go on," he prompted.

"Sometimes Papa received quite a big cheque. At others he used to get despondent when everything he wrote was refused, but somehow we managed."

There was a faint smile on her lips as she remembered happier times.

"And then your mother died?" the Duke prompted.

"Papa was lost without her. I tried to look after him, but he found it difficult to concentrate on his work. He became more and more depressed."

There was a tragic expression on her face and then she said, little above a whisper:

"I . . . I . . . think he . . . drowned . . . himself!"

"What do you mean—you think?" the Duke asked.

"It could . . . never be proved, but he went for a . . . swim at night . . . something he had never done before and he chose a part of the . . . river which was known to be . . . treacherous. All we . . . found were his . . . clothes on the . . . bank, and the body was . . . recovered . . . four days later!"

Selina clasped her fingers together and the Duke knew that she was fighting against her tears.

"I am sorry to make you tell me this when you have been through so much already," he said in a deep voice, "but you will understand I had to know?"

"Yes, of course," Selina agreed. "It is just that I can hardly . . . believe that I will never see . . . Papa again, or that he could have left me . . . alone."

"Perhaps it really was an accident!" the Duke said kindly.

"That is what I pretend to myself," Selina said, "and that is what the Coroner told me to believe."

"What happened after the funeral?" the Duke asked.

"I realised that I had to earn some money," Selina explained. "The cottage cost five shillings per week."

"Your parents had rented it?"

"Yes, and as we had lived there so many years the rent had never been increased. I wanted to go on living there but the Rector told me that people would talk about me as I was so young."

"Surely you could have gone to your mother's relations?"

"Mama had never communicated with them and they had made no attempt to find her after she ran away. I could not believe they would welcome me, and in any case for all I know they may be dead by now."

"What did you do?" the Duke asked.

"I went to London to try to sell some of Papa's music. He had written a great deal that he had never shown to anyone. There were also his compositions which had been refused but which I thought might be of interest. Tastes change, as Papa himself often said."

"So you went to London?"

"Yes. I knew the names of a few of the Agencies that Papa had been to and felt they would remember him."

"What happened?" the Duke asked.

"I went to one place off Piccadilly Circus. The man was very kind and said he was not interested at the moment but I should try another Agency a little further down the road. I did as he suggested but again the man there sent me to someone else."

Her eyes darkened and she ceased speaking.

"Tell me what happened," the Duke asked quietly.

"It was a rather scruffy, dirty place on the second floor," Selina said. "There was a fat man sitting at a desk and another man sitting beside him. They both looked at me in a way I did not like, but I told them why I had come and opened the satchel in which I had Papa's music.

"The fat man at the desk looked at it and then he said:

" 'I seem to know the name. Why has he not brought the music himself?'

"I told him Papa was dead and he seemed sympathetic although I thought it rather impertinent that he should ask so many questions. The other man seemed interested too."

"What was he like?" the Duke asked.

"He was a foreigner, dark and rather good-looking. I think now he was an . . . Arab!"

"It is more than likely," the Duke remarked.

"The dark man said he would like to hear the music but as there was no piano in the office he asked if I would mind coming with him so that I could play it for him."

"And you agreed?"

"He seemed quite pleasant," Selina replied. "When we got into a hired carriage he asked me whether I had ever thought of appearing on the stage and if I was good enough to give a performance on the piano.

"I told him I had no wish to do either of those things but he said he had a very good job to offer for someone like me but it would be abroad.

"I told him firmly that I could not possibly become a professional pianist and that all I wanted to do was sell Papa's music.

" 'I am sure I will be able to buy it,' he said.

"Although I did not like him, that was all that mattered. Then the carriage stopped and I saw to my surprise that we were near the river and there were buildings on one side of the road which looked like docks."

She paused before she continued:

"I suppose if I had had any sense I would have run away there and then, but I still thought he intended to buy Papa's music and I needed the money so desperately."

"What happened then?" the Duke asked.

"We went into a house . . . at least it seemed to be nothing more than a warehouse filled with packing-cases and boxes. Two youths were moving things about.

"The dark man led the way upstairs to a Sitting-

Room and I could see there was a bed-room opening off of it."

"Was it well furnished?" the Duke asked.

"I can hardly remember," Selina replied. "There was a sofa and some chairs. It looked rather sordid and yet in a way was quite expensive, if you know what I mean. It was certainly not in good taste."

"I understand," the Duke said. "What happened then?"

"The first thing I realised was that there was no piano in the room," Selina replied. "I thought it odd, but he said at once:

" 'The piano is in the flat upstairs but belongs to a friend of mine. I have to ask his permission to use it. Sit down and I will get you a cup of coffee while you are waiting.'

"I did as he said and he left me alone. I started to take out of the satchel the music I thought he would like to hear. I was sure he would not be interested in anything classical but would perhaps buy some of the songs Papa had written years ago which sounded tuneful and gay.

"I had been sorting them for a few minutes when the door opened and one of the young men I had seen downstairs came in with a cup of coffee.

"He put it down beside me and said:

" 'The Gov'nor says he'll be down in a jiffy! You're to drink this up so's you won't feel nervous. He's got several people up there he thinks might be interested in your music!' "

Selina gave a little sigh.

"Of course I felt excited and pleased at the idea of there being several people besides the dark man to listen to what Papa had written.

"I began to plan how wonderful it would be to go back to Coombe-on-Avon with enough money to last me for quite a long time."

"You drank the coffee?" the Duke asked.

"I drank it!" Selina answered, "and that is the last thing I remember. When I woke up I was on . . . board a . . . ship."

Her voice died away, then with a little murmur she put her hands up to her face.

"It was . . . horrible! T-terrifying!"

"Did you realise what had happened?" the Duke enquired.

"I felt so . . . ill. My head ached and my mouth was dry. . . . For a moment I could only think I had had an accident and been run down in the street, but then I saw there were other girls in the cabin. There were three of them lying on the bunks, two opposite and one above me . . . and they were asleep . . . at least I thought they were!"

Selina gave a little sob.

"Eventually I began to realise that something ghastly had happened and yet I could not imagine what it was."

"When did you begin to learn that you had been kidnapped?"

"Later . . . much later," Selina answered. "While I was looking round the dark man came into the cabin and there was another man with him.

" 'What has happened? Why am I here?' I asked. I expect I sounded hysterical.

" 'It's all right,' he said quietly. 'There has just been a mistake!'

" 'What sort of mistake?' I questioned.

" 'I will tell you about it,' he said, 'but first I expect your mouth is dry and you'd like a drink.'

"I saw that the other man carried a tray on which there were four mugs. He gave me one and said pleasantly: 'Drink it up and then we will have a talk.'

"Then he and the other man went to the other bunks and started pouring what was in the mugs down the girls' throats."

"Were they awake?" the Duke asked.

"The man shook one until she began to speak, then he put the mug to her lips and she drank quickly."

"And you drank what was in your mug?"

"Yes, I drank it down and I know now I must have slept for at least twenty-four hours."

"What happened after that?"

"When I woke up I was determined not to be taken in again.

"I realised that if I pretended to be asleep they would awaken me and force me to drink whatever was in the mugs. I therefore stayed awake and they allowed me to hold the mug.

"As soon as they were occupied with the other girls I tipped the contents of the mug down the back of the bunk, then I closed my eyes and pretended to go to sleep."

"For how long did this go on?" the Duke asked.

"I have no idea. It was difficult to guage time because the drugs I had already taken were so potent that anyway I kept falling asleep.

"I think it was when we had nearly reached Algiers that they decided to change their tactics.

"We were told to get up and dress and when we were on our feet they gave us a different sort of drug. It was a white powder and the other girls seemed to wake up and get very excited."

"You did not take it?" the Duke asked.

"I pretended to," Selina answered, "and because they thought I was quiet and manageable they did not trouble themselves with me.

"The German girls made a terrible fuss at something the men told them. One of them screamed and tried to throw herself overboard."

Her voice dropped.

"That was when they . . . beat her. It was . . . horrible! I shall . . . hear her . . . screaming for the rest of my . . . life."

"You will forget it," the Duke said quietly. "When did they tell you what was going to happen to you?"

"They told me nothing!" Selina answered. "And as I could not speak the language of the other girls I could not find out what they thought was happening to them."

She hesitated and then said:

"I imagined I had been kidnapped but I did not know why. I thought people were kidnapped only because they were rich and could pay for their release."

"That is the usual reason," the Duke said.

"I told myself I must try to escape, and I was determined not to take the drugs they kept giving us."

"You now realised the other girls were drugged?"

"It made them behave so strangely," Selina answered. "They would laugh and dance about, kiss each other and sing. It was all dreadfully unnatural. I was terrified of behaving like that."

"How did you prevent them from being suspicious?" the Duke asked.

"I kept on talking about playing the piano, as if that had remained in my mind," Selina replied. "I talked and talked whenever they appeared and once the dark man said in French to the man who was with him: 'Funny how it takes them! I should have thought she would have been the laughing sort!'

" 'We've got enough of those on our hands!' the other man said, and it was true.

"The German girls laughed and laughed until it was frightening."

Selina paused for a moment and then she said:

"One difficulty was that I dared not eat anything. I knew they could put drugs in the drinks and I suspected it was also in the food."

"No wonder you look so thin!" the Duke said.

"I was too frightened to be hungry anyway!" Selina answered.

"When you reached Algiers you were taken straight to the house where I saw you?"

"We were driven there in a closed carriage and told not to look out of the windows.

"We had to walk the last part of the way up the steps and there were four or five men who hurried us up them."

Selina paused, then in a whisper she added:

"That was . . . all that . . . happened! I cannot . . . I cannot . . . tell you any . . . more!"

Chapter Four

"I have never had a more wonderful meal!" Selina exclaimed as dinner was finished and the stewards withdrew from the Saloon.

"I am glad you enjoyed it," the Duke replied.

"If I ate like this every day I would soon get fat!"

"You have a long way to go before you need worry about that!" the Duke smiled.

They had risen from the table and seated themselves in two comfortable arm-chairs at the other end of the Saloon.

Decorated in pale green with exquisite prints on the walls, it seemed very unlike a ship and Selina had already told the Duke how attractive she thought it was.

Sitting back with a glass of brandy in his hand and Selina opposite him, the Duke thought that despite her peasant-dress she looked like a nymph that might have risen from the sea.

All day they had steamed amongst the Balearic Islands and she had been entranced with everything she saw.

"I always thought the islands of the Mediterranean would look like this!" she said. Then quietly, almost beneath her breath, she quoted:

> " 'To see the mountains kiss high Heaven
> And the waves clasp one another . . .' "

She paused, then added:

"Tonight I shall expect to see 'the moonbeams kiss the sea'!"

The Duke recognised the lines from Shelley and said with a smile:

"I am beginning to suspect that you think in poetry!"

"Sometimes," she admitted.

"You read a lot of it?"

"Papa always thought that poetry said in words what music tried to say in sound. I used to read to him when he was composing something new in his mind. He said it inspired him!"

"I am sure it did!" the Duke replied. "And does it inspire you?"

"I do not know quite what it would inspire me to do. I am not talented like Papa," Selina replied. "But it always makes me think of beautiful things and I suppose in a way it makes me understand the world better."

Again the Duke waited for an explanation and she said a little hesitantly:

"I try . . . to understand why the countryside is so . . . beautiful at every Season of the year and I try too to find . . . beauty in people."

She spoke quite simply and without the slightest touch of affectation.

Looking at her now, the Duke could not help thinking what a strange day it had been.

He had never before been alone with a woman who had not tried to attract him.

The women he knew used every artifice to flirt, beguile, and entertain him.

If they did not flirt in words they flirted with their eyes, with their lips, with every movement of their bodies.

All the time he was with them he was made vividly conscious that he was a man and they were of the opposite sex.

He had not believed it possible that he could talk with a woman very much in the same way that he talked with Nicholas Vlastov.

He had found that conversation, except with his friend, began with himself and the woman concerned and ended in exactly the same way.

He was also well aware that if he had been alone on his yacht with any of the sophisticated, fascinating, and beautiful women he knew, by this time the fire of desire would be rising within them both and it would only be a question of time before they were in each other's arms.

Selina talked to him with a frankness and a child-like simplicity but there was nothing child-like about her intelligence.

He realised that while her life had been so limited she had with her father and mother studied so many subjects that he had never expected a woman to know about.

What was more, she had read extensively Greek mythology, the Classics, and especially poetry.

It was impossible to talk to her without being aware of how innocent she was about the world and yet strangely enough she was not particularly curious about it.

She had, he realised, no idea of how important he was or that most women would deem it not only a privilege but an opportunity to be alone with him in his yacht.

"Have you travelled a great deal?" she asked him. "Please tell me about it."

Because, as Nicholas had said, the Duke had travelled only rather grandly, dependent on the privilege of his rank, he felt almost ashamed that he could not tell her that he had journeyed to strange, mysterious places no other man had explored.

He found himself quite irrationally wishing that he had attempted to reach the sacred city of Lhasa in Tibet, crossed the Gobi Desert, or sailed up the Amazon.

Instead he told her about China when he went round the world after leaving Oxford and of India, where he had been entertained by the Viceroy.

"Did you see any Sadhus or Holy-men?" Selina asked.

The Duke searched his mind and had to admit that they had not been present at the innumerable parties that had been given for him, on the tiger-shoots arranged by the Maharajas, or in the impressive Government Houses at which he had stayed in various parts of the country.

"I have heard of them," he conceded, "but I believe most of them live in the foot-hills of the Himalayas or in some inaccessible spot where only their disciples can find them."

"I have read the life of Buddha," Selina said, "and feel there is so much knowledge hidden in the East that would help people to live at peace with each other."

"Mankind is always engaged in wars of some sort," the Duke said lightly.

"Wars are brutal and barbarous!" Selina retorted.

She spoke with a note in her voice which made the Duke know that she was sensitive and very vulnerable to anything that appertained to cruelty.

He could not help wondering if the terrifying experience of being kidnapped and taken to Algiers would leave an inerasable scar upon her mind for the rest of her life.

Then he told himself that while it might make her nervous and wary, like a high-strung animal that had been harshly treated, she also had so much intelligence that she would in time force herself to think of it calmly.

At the moment she was taut and on edge.

It was nothing that she said in so many words that made him think this, merely the fact that he found himself sensing intuitively what she was thinking even when she did not speak.

It had been a day of sunshine and when they came back to the yacht, having explored one of the tiny islands, Selina carried some wild flowers, which she gave to Gregson to put in a vase in the Saloon.

"I think you are tired," the Duke said now, after they had not spoken for some minutes.

"I am a little," Selina confessed.

"Then go to bed," he said. "You have a lot of sleep to make up, and very early tomorrow morning we shall move towards Monte Carlo."

Her eyes went to his quickly and he saw a question in them.

"I do not wish you to go straight back to England," he said, "but until we have made plans as to what you can do and where you should stay, I do not think you would wish to be alone at your cottage."

"I . . . I do not think I would really be . . . frightened," Selina said, "not at . . . home, but . . ."

There was a silence and the Duke said after a moment:

"Finish the sentence!"

"I must . . . find some . . . work to . . . do."

"This is something we can talk about later," the Duke said. "I am going to take you to my Villa at Monte Carlo. There is someone staying there who will chaperon you and whom I think you will like."

He thought that Selina looked a little wary and he said:

"She is an old lady. She was a friend of my mother's and every year she comes to stay with me at Monte Carlo for three months."

"If she looks forward to staying with you," Selina said, "she might find a stranger a nuisance!"

The Duke smiled.

"I am sure Mrs. Sherman will be delighted to see you," he said reassuringly, "and perhaps you will have something in common. She was a famous painter of miniatures, which was how my mother met her.

"She came to Atherstone Castle when I was a little boy to paint a miniature of me. Her work was so exquisite that my mother became her friend and brought her a great many Commissions so that she became in fact quite famous!"

"Does she still paint?" Selina asked.

The Duke shook his head.

"As she grew older she had arthritis in her hands and so she could no longer use them."

He did not add that Mrs. Sherman had managed to save very little money and it was only her being his guest for three months of the year which made it possible for her to live in comparative comfort for the rest of the time.

"I would love to meet her," Selina said, "as long as you are quite certain she does not wish to be alone with you."

The Duke smiled to himself at the naiveté of it.

What would Selina have thought, he wondered, of the smart, gay, witty people whom he had told Colonel Grayson to send away from the Villa?

And what indeed would she think of Lady Millie? Or Lady Millie of her?

Selina went to bed and the Duke sat on in the Saloon thinking.

He was well aware that on returning to Monte Carlo quite a number of problems awaited him.

However important he might be socially he had still behaved with unprecedented rudeness in turning his guests out of the Villa without an explanation or an apology.

He told himself now that the only guest he had really wanted to be rid of was Lady Millie because she had annoyed him.

Also he had no intention of allowing her to dominate him as she was trying to do.

The fact that they all had to leave might have softened the blow; nevertheless he was quite certain that she would demand to see him on his return and undoubtedly make a scene.

As he thought of it he knew that his mind was made up. His affair with Lady Millie was finished!

It had been finished, he thought, although he would not admit it to himself, before he came to Monte Carlo, which was why he had felt a sudden distaste for all the secrecy and the subterfuge which had been so much a part of the liaison.

He had endured it before, but as Nicholas Vlastov had said:

"Passion dies!"

Lady Millie, although he had thought differently at first, was just another flower by the road-side!

At the same time he could not help feeling that the part he had played in their love-affair was not particularly to his credit.

And yet, he consoled himself, Lady Millie, sophisticated and a woman of the world, was not a girl whom he had seduced from the path of virtue.

He was not the first lover nor was there any likelihood of his being the last, but she had undoubtedly visualised herself as becoming the Duchess of Atherstone!

Perhaps he had, without expressing it in words, raised her hopes and led her to think that he would in fact marry her.

He wondered how much Lady Millie really cared for him as a man apart from the trappings of a Ducal coronet and his much envied possessions.

He remembered long ago when he was only just in his teens his mother saying to him:

"I hope one day, Draco darling, you will find someone who will really love you and whom you will love with all your heart."

They had been speaking of a Royal marriage that had just taken place where the bride-groom was very old and the bride barely out of the School-Room.

The Duke had asked ingenuously, just as Selina might have done:

"Do you think they will be happy, Mama?"

It was then that his mother had said the words to him which he had never forgotten and which he thought now must always have been at the back of his mind during his relationships with many women.

He had a feeling that his mother had been afraid that he might be propelled into matrimony just because of his Social importance.

"Mama would not have approved of Millie!" the Duke told himself.

He knew that all older women disapproved of the way she flaunted her beauty provocatively, sometimes outrageously.

It was not only what she did or the way she looked.

It was as if the withered, dried-up old Dowagers seated on the dais at Balls sensed her voluptuousness, the insatiable fire within her, and the unbridled passion which exceeded anything he had ever found in any other woman.

No, the Duke told himself again, his mother would not have approved of Millie, and certainly not as his wife!

Yet sooner or later, he realised, he had to marry.

He must have an heir, for one thing, and sometimes when he was not surrounded by crowds of friends he found it lonely.

There were moments when he would ride in the morning over the park-land or through the woods at Atherstone Castle, on the superlative horses on which he spent a fortune, when he would have liked a companion with him.

He wanted to talk to someone who cared of the Estate which was a part of himself, the improvements he wished to make, and the problems which only he could solve.

It would be nice, he had thought sometimes, to have children, who he could teach to ride as his father had taught him.

A son who would go out shooting with him; who would accompany him when he fished for trout that filled the great lake.

But these had been only passing fantasies in the past and he had not dwelt on them.

Now he knew that each one of them had influenced his decision not to marry Lady Millie.

Perhaps, he told himself, it was his talk with Nicholas Vlastov that had finally decided him, although the actual break had come the moment he walked away from her in the Casino.

It had been such a little sentence to end a love-affair which had lasted for so long and which had so very nearly finished with the conventional wedding-bells.

"At least you are—rich!"

He could hear her saying it, see the smouldering resentment in her eyes and the bitter curve of her red lips.

It had been a deliberate blow dealt by one who knew that to the man she was trying to hurt it would be like the thrust of a dagger.

Lady Millie was well aware that he was sensitive on the point of having so much wealth and so much prestige, that he wanted to be loved for himself.

She knew that sometimes, like a Prince in a fairy-tale, he longed to be incognito and find that it was not the Royal aura which mattered but just his heart.

They had sometimes laughed together when people exaggerated their deference to him because he was a Duke; when women fawned upon him simply because they were snobs.

But from the time Lady Millie was free, although he would not admit it, the Duke found himself wondering whether she would be so anxious to marry him if he were just a commoner of no importance.

She desired him as a man—of that he was in no doubt—but whether she loved him was a very different thing.

Then, he asked himself simply, was love really important enough to ignore the trappings which made life comfortable, the wealth which ensured no worry about the future?

Where Nicholas Vlastov and Fatimat were concerned nothing had been of the slightest consequence but their love for each other.

He could remember now the horrified comments of the Social world when it was learnt that they had left Russia, that Nicholas had resigned from his position as a Diplomat, and that Fatimat's husband was saying openly that he intended to kill him in a duel.

What made their behaviour worse was that Nicholas did not remain to fight the duel, which he should have done according to the demands of the then-accepted code of honour.

The two of them had just vanished—no-one knew where.

For nearly a year it seemed as if the whole world was being combed for them. Then the Duke received a letter which made him proceed immediately to Algiers.

He found them living in one small room in a state of poverty, which had seemed to him at first quite horrifying.

Then he had realised that, incredibly, they were blissfully, ecstatically happy.

He had never believed that two people could radiate such contentment.

Their love shone in their faces, in every word they spoke, in the manner in which Nicholas would reach out to take Fatimat's hand, as if every moment he had to reassure himself that she was there beside him.

The Duke had left Algiers with the manuscript of Nicholas's first book in a state of questioning surprise.

Was it possible that two people who had known the luxury, the comfort, and the amusements of the Cosmopolitan world could be content with no money in one tiny, squalid little room?

However much he questioned it the answer was quite simple.

It was "Yes!"

The Duke stretched his legs and realised that he had been sitting for a very long time in the Saloon and it was time that he went to bed.

He had told Gregson not to wait up for him and now he extinguished the lights and walked along the passage to his cabin.

He moved quietly so as not to disturb Selina, although he expected she would sleep as deeply as she had done last night when he had gone into her cabin and it had not disturbed her.

His own cabin was a masterpiece not only of comfort but also of ingenuity.

He had thought up so many gadgets, so many little extras that could be built into the yacht that the builder had exclaimed in admiration:

"Your Grace could make a fortune if you became an Architect and Designer!"

"Perhaps I will consider it one day," the Duke smiled.

"You should certainly patent these new ideas of yours."

The Duke had laughed.

"Let anyone have them who needs them."

"You're giving away a fortune!" the builder had expostulated.

"Why not?" the Duke enquired.

It had been an easy gesture because he could well afford it.

It gave him a great deal of satisfaction to know that he could turn a switch or a knob and produce an effect that no-one had thought of before.

It had also made his yacht the most talked-of privately owned vessel in the whole of Great Britain.

The Duke had taken off his velvet smoking-jacket and was standing in his shirt-sleeves when he heard a cry.

For a moment he started, then he thought it must have come from the sea-gulls who had flown round the yacht all day, screaming as if in disapproval as they left the harbour and entered another.

The cry came again and he knew now that it came from next door.

Hastily he went from his own cabin and opened the door of Selina's. The room was in darkness and for a moment he thought that he must have been mistaken.

Then before he could switch on the light something warm, soft, and terrified flung itself against him.

His arms went round her as she cried:

"Save me! Save me! They are . . . trying to . . . catch me. Save me!"

He could feel her hands clutching frantically at his shirt and her body beneath the soft silk which covered her was trembling as she had trembled last night when he had lifted her down from one roof after another.

"It is all right, Selina," he said quietly, "you are safe."

"They . . . will . . . catch me!" she murmured, her face hidden against his shoulder.

"Wake up! You are dreaming!" he commanded. "There is no-one trying to catch you."

It was as if his words got through to her, but she still clung to him and was still trembling, her whole body shaking in a manner which told him the desperation of her feelings.

"You have been having a nightmare," he said gently. "They are very unpleasant, but they have no substance in fact."

"I thought . . . they were . . . going to . . . catch

me," Selina said in a whisper. "They were . . . reaching out!"

"Forget it!" the Duke said.

"It was . . . horrible!"

"I am sure it was, but now you are awake, you know it was only your imagination!"

His words seemed to be having the right effect and she was not trembling as violently as she had been, but she still held on to him.

"Are you quite . . . sure they . . . cannot come after me . . . they are not . . . hiding somewhere where we . . . cannot see them?"

"I am quite sure that *'they'* are in Algiers and you and I are here with an English crew to guard us most effectively!"

He felt her give a deep sigh.

"I am being . . . foolish," she murmured.

"You are getting cold," the Duke replied in a practical voice. "I suggest you get back into bed."

"You will not . . . leave me?"

"No, of course not."

Hesitatingly she released his shirt, which she had clutched in her frenzy, and almost reluctantly she turned towards the bed.

The Duke guided her and with one hand reached out and switched on the lamp.

As he did so Selina slipped beneath the bed-clothes.

The face she turned towards him was very pale and he could see that the terror still lingered in her eyes.

He sat down on the edge of the bed, facing her.

"I promise you that you are completely and absolutely safe."

"That is what I . . . told myself . . . today," she said. "I was so . . . happy and it was so . . . wonderful seeing the islands and being at sea, but . . ."

The Duke waited for her to go on. It was as if she found difficulty in finding the words.

Then suddenly they came in a rush, falling over each other:

"I shall . . . never feel . . . safe again. Never! Never!"

"You are frightening yourself," the Duke said quietly. "Think it out logically, Selina. You have a good brain and you can do that."

Her eyes were on his and he continued, still in the calm voice that he had used when she had clung to him:

"The men have been paid and they have not lost so very much over the transaction, so they will not feel as bitter or revengful as they might."

As he spoke Selina's hand crept out and her fingers slid into his.

It was, he knew, a desire to hold on to something solid; to be quite certain that he was real and she was not still dreaming.

He covered her cold fingers with both of his hands and went on:

"There are a great many more women in the world, and they would be very stupid to worry their heads too much over just one who slipped through the net."

"You are . . . right, of course," Selina said in a breathless voice. "At the same . . . time I am . . . frightened. I cannot . . . help it. I am . . . frightened!"

"I know you are. Shall I get you something to drink?"

"No! No! Do not . . . leave me," she begged.

Her fingers clung to his desperately and he said reassuringly:

"I have already told you that I will not leave you, not until you want me to."

"I must not be a . . . nuisance," she murmured.

"You have never been that," the Duke said, "and I think that when we are old we shall talk of what has happened as a very exciting adventure. After all, we won! Do not forget that, Selina, we won!"

"You . . . saved me! If it had not . . . been for . . . you . . ."

"Forget it!" the Duke said. "I told you to forget it!"

"I am trying to," Selina answered, "but there is one . . . thing I do not . . . understand."

"What is that?"

She bent her head and her hair fell forward as it had the night before when she had stood in the line with the other girls.

"I do not . . . know quite how to . . . tell you," she whispered.

"Well, suppose we make it easier."

He rose off the bed as he spoke and shut the cabin-door. Then he sat down beside Selina with his back against the pillows.

"Now," he said, "I am quite prepared to stay here as long as you want me to do so."

As he spoke very gently, so as not to frighten her, he put his arm round her shoulders.

He felt her stiffen for a moment but he knew that it was in surprise, not because she resented his touch. Then with a little sigh she bent her head against his shoulder.

"It is easy to talk like . . . this," she said, "and I would not . . . want you to be . . . uncomfortable."

The Duke could not help thinking with a slightly amused smile that no other woman of his acquaintance would have accepted such a situation in such a matter-of-fact manner.

He realised, as he had done all day, that Selina treated him very much the same way that she must have treated her father.

She gave him companionship, and not even at this moment did she appear to think of him as being a young man or even—a sobering thought—attractive from a masculine point of view.

"What do you not understand?" the Duke asked in a deep voice.

"It is very puzzling," Selina answered. "When we reached that house last night there was a terrible commotion because the ship had been late and they were expecting us several days earlier."

She paused.

"Anyway, we were told to have a bath quickly

and there were Arab women to wash our hair. One of the women spoke French."

"That was the first time you had been able to talk to anybody or to understand them?" the Duke asked.

"I could understand the dark man who had said he wanted to buy Papa's music because he always spoke French, except to the servants, but I could not converse with any of the girls."

"Go on."

"The Arab woman talked a little French, and it was she who told me, when I asked her, that we were in Algiers."

"You had not realised that before?"

"No," Selina answered. "When I knew that that was where I was, I was terrified."

"Of the place?" the Duke asked.

"Yes, because I had read about the Barbary pirates who had kept Christian slaves in Algiers, and I began to think that that was the reason why we had been brought there."

The Duke was silent and after a moment she went on:

"I was sure of it when I had some scented oil rubbed on my skin and in my hair."

The Duke had noticed that she smelt of jasmin when he had been lifting her from roof to roof and he could smell it still now that her head was on his shoulder.

"Then they gave us those indecent gauze gowns," Selina went on, blushing, "and I was quite certain I was right and we were to go to a Slave-Market . . . and when we were brought into the room . . . where you were . . . I was sure of it."

"You looked very frightened," the Duke said.

"We had all been given the . . . white powder to take before we went in. Once again I pretended to take mine and they had no idea that I had not done so."

"So you expected to be in a Slave-Market," the Duke prompted.

"I thought that that was why they had taken away our clothes," Selina said in a low voice. "Because

I had read that slaves were always sold . . . naked."

"Did you understand why?"

"In a book I read it was to see how . . . strong they were and it said that the weakest became servants, doing all the menial jobs for the Officials and their wives, while the stronger men were made to mine granite, build houses, or help in the ship-yards."

"So you expected to be a servant?"

"Yes, of course," Selina answered. "Then when we came into the room I heard the Patron say, 'Let me remind Your Excellencies that you cannot take the women from the house.' "

She paused and then asked hesitatingly:

"How could we work as . . . servants if we had to stay where we were? And why when a girl was sold did she go up to a . . . bed-room, and the man who had . . . bought . . . her . . . follow her?"

The Duke did not answer and after a moment she said:

"The Arab women had said that the bed-room you . . . found me in was . . . mine, but . . . you came . . . there. How was I expected to . . . work for . . . you?"

For a moment the Duke could not realise that she really did not understand.

Then he knew that someone who had been brought up in the country and was completely and absolutely innocent would have no idea what the house was or the fact that such places existed.

The difficulty was for him to tell Selina the truth without frightening her more than she was already.

He thought that perhaps he should say nothing, and then he knew that that would not only be an insult to her intelligence, but she would go on wondering about it and turning it over in her mind.

She was waiting and as he did not speak she said:

"Perhaps I should not have . . . asked you. There was something so . . . evil, so . . . wicked, in the . . . atmosphere of the house that it may be . . . something of which you would not wish . . . to speak."

"I want to tell you the truth," the Duke replied, "but once you know it I want you to erase from your mind everything that happened since you went to London to sell your father's music."

He paused, then asked:

"If I tell you what you want to know will you try to forget, as I have asked you to do?"

"I promise . . . you I will . . . try, I promise you on my . . . honour."

Again the Duke found it difficult to find the words until at last he said:

"When you read the story of the Barbary pirates and the seamen they captured from the ships and made into slaves, was there any reference to the women amongst them, who must have often been on the passenger-vessels?"

Selina thought.

"I suppose they must have written about the women slaves, but it was a very old book and rather difficult to read."

She was silent for a moment, thinking before she said:

"It did say that the Dey was entitled to chose any of the slaves that he particularly wanted for himself and that he sometimes sent them as presents to the Sultan of Turkey."

"Turkey is full of men, the Sultan would have had all he wanted," the Duke said.

"Then it would have been . . . women that were sent to the . . . Sultan."

"Yes."

"But why?"

"To add to his Harem. The Sultan of Turkey had hundreds, if not thousands, of women in his Harem."

Selina drew in a deep breath, and as if she could not help herself she once again put one hand into the Duke's.

"Do you mean," she asked in a very low voice, "that these . . . Sheiks last night were . . . buying the girls for their . . . Harems?"

"That was the reason they were there," the Duke answered, "only instead of taking them away they were to be left in the house so that they could visit them whenever they wished to do so."

Selina's fingers tightened on his until the pressure of them hurt.

"Then if you had not . . . bought me," she whispered, "I would have . . . belonged to one of those . . ."

She gave a little cry and turned her face towards the Duke's shoulder.

"It . . . is . . . horrible! Beastly! I had no . . . idea that anything like . . . that could . . . happen in the world today!"

He held her close and after a moment said in his calm, quiet voice:

"The world alters very little, Selina, and you have read enough to know that Solomon had a great many concubines; that Sultans all through the ages have filled their Harems with pretty women. What you do not know is that there are always places like the one you were in last night, which cater to men who want to be entertained and amused outside their home."

"But surely . . . only in the . . . East," Selina said.

"In the West too—in London and Paris and all the great cities of the world," the Duke answered quietly.

"I could not imagine such a thing," Selina exclaimed. "I only knew I was . . . frightened. I thought I might be . . . beaten . . . ill-treated as the slaves had been in the past. To be in a . . . Harem . . . that I . . . never . . . imagined!"

"You promised me if I told you the truth you would not go on thinking about it," the Duke said. "It is something that will never happen to you again!"

Her face was still against his shoulder and after a moment she said in a muffled voice:

"How . . . do you . . . know? How . . . can I . . . ever go to . . . London? How can I live . . . alone if I am afraid there will be . . . men?"

There was so much logic in what she said that the Duke found it difficult to know what to answer. Then after a moment he said:

"You have to trust me in this, Selina. We are going to talk about your future when we get to Monte Carlo. I wanted you first to get over the shock of what you have been through."

She did not reply and he knew that she was breathing in a frightened manner.

He could feel her heart beating against his through the thin silk she wore and the soft linen of his shirt.

"All men . . . cannot be like . . . that," she said after a moment. "Not Papa! . . . not . . . you!"

"No, of course not," the Duke answered soothingly, and hoped he would be forgiven for lying.

"I shall have to . . . earn my living . . . somehow."

There was a desperate sound to the words.

"I told you that we will discuss it later," the Duke said. "I am asking you to trust me, Selina. Surely after all we have been through you can do that?"

She raised her face and he saw a smile on her lips as she said:

"You know I trust you. You have been so wonderful, so unbelievably wonderful to me. How lucky I am that you were there last night."

She paused, the smile faded from her lips, and there was a sudden question in her eyes.

"Why . . . were you . . . there?"

"I was there because, like you, I did not believe that such things really happened," the Duke answered. "I had a friend with me who is a very famous writer. He told me that the Slave-Market still existed in Algiers, just as it had done in the past. I told him he was exaggerating and so he took me along as a spectator."

He smiled.

"That was all I intended to be, but you know the trouble in which you involved me!"

"I am so glad . . . so very glad!" Selina exclaimed. "But if you had not been clever enough to find the trap-door in the ceiling, I would have still been a prisoner in that . . . terrible . . . house. . . ."

"You are breaking your promise," the Duke said warningly.

"Yes . . . I know."

"I kept my part of the bargain."

Selina gave a deep sigh.

"I will . . . try, but it will be difficult not to . . . think about . . . it."

"You gave me your word of honour!"

"Yes, I know, and Papa said that once one had given a word of honour it was a sacred bond and must never be . . . broken."

"Then keep to it!"

"I promise. I promise to do what you . . . want me to . . . do."

"Now I think you ought to go to sleep," the Duke said. "Again you are sensible enough to realise that having taken the drugs they gave you and no food for so long, your body has to grow strong again, just as your mind has to be strong enough to forget all that frightened you."

"You sound like a Doctor!"

"It is exactly what I am—a Doctor of health!" the Duke said. "So you are not to worry, Selina. If I had not been healthy and very strong we should not be sitting here at this moment."

"You opened the trap-door," Selina murmured almost beneath her breath. "You knocked down that man who was following us. Yes, you are very . . . strong."

"Tomorrow, if it is warm enough," the Duke said in a matter-of-fact tone, "I am going to swim in the sea before we arrive in Monte Carlo."

He felt a little shiver run through her as she said apprehensively:

"You will be . . . safe?"

He knew that she was thinking of her father and he said quickly:

"I assure you I am a very strong swimmer, and you shall watch me from the yacht and throw me a life-buoy if there is any danger of my sinking."

He saw that she was reassured and he said with a twist to his lips:

"I have the feeling that you are worrying not so much about my being in danger but the fact that if I drown there will be no one to look after you!"

"I was really thinking of you," Selina answered, "but now that you say that . . . please . . . please go on looking . . . after me, but only until you have found me some . . . work so that I can make some . . . money and look after myself."

"I see I have a grave responsibility where you are

concerned," the Duke said. "You know there is an old legend that if you save someone's life you can never be rid of him."

"I . . . hope I am not going . . . to be like . . . that."

She looked at him a little nervously, as if she felt that she was presuming on his kindness.

"I have already told you," the Duke said, "that I accept my responsibilities for having rescued you."

Again Selina gave a sigh.

"You too need your rest. I am not . . . frightened . . . anymore."

The Duke rose and took his arm from her shoulders.

"You are really no longer afraid?" he asked.

"If I am . . . can I come . . . to you?"

Just for a moment he wondered what construction his Social friends would put on such an artless remark, then he answered gravely:

"Of course, you know I am only next door. If you call out I shall hear you."

"Thank you," Selina said in a soft, breathless voice. "It is such an . . . inadequate word . . . but thank you so very, very . . . much for . . . everything."

Chapter Five

When Selina woke they were in harbour. She looked out of the port-hole and saw that Monte Carlo was far more impressive than she had ever imagined.

She dressed as quickly as she could in her peasant-costume and hurried to the Saloon. The Duke was already there and he rose as she entered, saying:

"Good morning, Selina. I thought perhaps you would be tired and sleep late."

"I am used to getting up early," Selina smiled.

The steward held a chair for her and she sat down at the table, then, finding it hard, she hesitated to choose from the numerous dishes—far more than she had ever thought anyone could be offered at breakfast.

"I have been making plans," the Duke said.

Selina looked up enquiringly and he went on:

"We will be staying at my Villa which is on the hill above Monte Carlo. But first as you will need clothes; I have sent Gregson to fetch one of the best dress-makers in the town. She will have some gowns already made up and we can order others. And you will also need a riding-habit."

Selina looked at him wide-eyed. Then she said:

"You must not spend too much money on me. As you well know, I wish to pay you . . . back."

"That is an action which I think we can leave to the future," the Duke replied with a smile.

"I cannot be . . . any more in your . . . debt."

He looked amused.

"Why not?" he asked.

"You have been so kind already. I know that you feel that, having . . . saved me, you must be . . . responsible for me. That does not necessarily mean I must be a very . . . expensive responsibility."

The Duke laughed.

"I assure you, Selina, you will not prove nearly so expensive as some of the women I have known in the past."

He spoke without thinking and then he noticed the expression on her face.

"I have numerous relations who all think of me as a kind of Father Christmas," he added quickly.

He saw the question in Selina's eyes vanish and he told himself that he must be careful—very careful of what he said to her.

He had never before been with anyone who was not only so unsophisticated but whose every emotion was mirrored in her eyes.

Selina's face was so expressive, so sensitive, that he told himself that it was almost like reading a book and that if he hurt her he would know immediately what he had done.

As they finished breakfast Gregson came into the Saloon to say:

"Madame Françoise is here, Your Grace."

"Show her in," the Duke commanded.

A middle-aged French woman appeared, plump and not particularly attractive, but it was impossible not to realise how smartly dressed she was.

Despite the fact that she had a bad figure on which to display her gown, everything about her cried *"chic."*

She wore a black-and-white striped dress with tiny touches of red, an impertinent little hat with several red quills perched on top of her head, and peeping beneath the hem of her gown there was a glimpse of red kid boots.

Madame Françoise swept a low curtsey.

"I am honoured by your patronage, *Monsieur le Duc,*" she said in French.

"And I am grateful to you, Madame, for coming here at short notice," the Duke replied. "This is Miss Gretton, my Ward, who requires a gown immediately in which she can go ashore, and several others if you have them which she can wear until those which must be made are completed."

"It is a pleasure, *Monsieur,*" Madame Françoise exclaimed.

Before Selina quite realised what was happening to her she was taken into her cabin and Madame Françoise had whisked a tape-measure round her, exclaiming with delight at the smallness of her waist.

At the same time Madame declared that her height was just right for the majority of her gowns, which were made for French women and not for the English, who were too tall!

She had brought with her, Selina found, a large number of boxes and two subservient, rather crushed young women who opened them on her orders, producing first gowns and then materials, almost as if they were rabbits out of a magician's hat.

Madame Françoise helped Selina into a dress of pale blue crepe trimmed with tiny rouchings of white muslin slotted through with velvet ribbon.

When it was buttoned up the back Selina looked at herself in the long mirror which was attached to one of the walls of her cabin and was astonished at her appearance.

Never before had she realised how classically perfect her figure could look in a fashionable dress moulded tightly over her breasts and draped exquisitely at the back.

"C'est ravissant!" Madame Françoise exclaimed.

"It is indeed very pretty," Selina said in a low voice. "But I am afraid it must be very expensive."

"That is not important," Madame Françoise replied loftily. "Will you not show yourself to *Monsieur le Duc* and ask his approval?"

"Yes, of course," Selina agreed.

She went from her cabin to the Saloon.

The Duke was sitting in one of the arm-chairs, reading a newspaper. He put it down when Selina appeared. He looked her over with what she thought was a critical eye.

"Do you like it?" she asked a little nervously. "You do not think it is too elaborate . . . too rich-looking for someone . . . like me?"

"I think it is charming," the Duke said. "Let me see some more."

Selina hesitated a moment as if she would say something and then she ran back to the cabin.

Now Madame Françoise dressed her in a gown of pale green, the colour of the Spring grass through which they had wandered on one of the small islands to pick the wild flowers she had brought back to the yacht.

The green dress also met with the Duke's approval.

Then Madame Françoise produced an evening gown which left Selina gasping. It was of gauze tulle and soft satin with a shimmer of tiny diamanté.

It was very young and at the same time it had that indefinable *chic* which only a French dress-maker can create.

"It is beautiful," Selina breathed, "but far too grand! I shall never have an occasion to wear a gown like this."

"Show it to *Monsieur le Duc,*" Madame Françoise suggested.

Selina went back to the Saloon.

Once again the Duke put down his newspaper.

"I am only showing you this," Selina explained, "because Madame Françoise insisted that I should. I quite realise that I shall never have the opportunity to wear anything so beautiful."

"How can you be so sure of that?" the Duke enquired.

Selina laughed.

"I cannot imagine that a teacher, or whatever other employment you intend to find me, would be expected to outshine her employer!"

"I think in that dress," the Duke said in his deep voice, "you would outshine anyone."

"You are teasing me," Selina said after a moment. "At the same time it is a very beautiful gown."

"Put on the dress you showed me first," the Duke said, "and send Madame to me."

Selina smiled.

"Please remember I have to have something practical, like a shawl," she said. "And shoes. I hate to remind you of these things. But they are necessities."

"I agree, you are very practical," the Duke said.

"In this dress," Selina answered, "I feel I could dance on the sea or fly up into the clouds, but I have to come down to earth and remember that I have to spend your money on rather mundane things like gloves and pocket handkerchiefs."

"I have not forgotten anything," the Duke replied. "I have, in fact, made a list of what I think you will require."

"May I see it?" Selina asked.

"No," he answered. "Because if I show it to you I feel sure you will bore me with worrying as to how you will manage to pay for it all! Let me assure you once again, Selina, I am well content to be your Banker."

"You are very generous," she said, "but at the same time I shall go on worrying."

She went from the Saloon and he looked after her with a smile on his face.

He wondered what she would say if he told her what the emerald necklace he had given Lady Millie for Christmas had cost!

He felt that she would be more shocked at the enormous bill for thousands of francs which had come from Worth's in Paris, where Lady Millie had spent three days en route to Monte Carlo.

She had taken it as a matter of course that he should pay for the elaborate and spectacular gowns from the most expensive *couturier* in all Europe that she was unable to afford herself.

Just as she had expected him to give her the sables she had desired at the beginning of the Winter, and innumerable other expensive objects, far too many for the Duke to remember.

He had never for a moment queried the fact that he should buy whatever his mistresses required of him.

There had been many women before Lady Millie who had sent him bills which had been so exorbitant that at times he had found himself thinking what excellent horse-flesh he could buy for himself for the same amount.

But he was a very rich man and if he could not

use his money to keep happy the women he favoured, what use was it?

This was the first time that any woman had ever suggested paying him back or urged economy.

It was true, however, that he could not put Selina, whose life had crossed his only by chance, in the same category as women who had been close to him for a very different reason.

At the same time it was a new experience and he found it rather touching.

He was determined all the same that Selina should have a large and attractive wardrobe in which she could face the world when he found her the sort of position in which she could support herself.

He admitted that was not going to be easy and he had puzzled his mind for many hours during the night as to what she could do.

She herself obviously expected something in the role of a teacher and that he supposed it would have to be.

There were only two professions open for ladies —that of being a companion or a governess. The Duke had seen the former attending some of his more awe-inspiring female relations.

Crushed, cowed little women, they appeared to shake with fright when he spoke to them and spend their lives slipping away like shadows when they were not required and being sharply reproved for not being present when they were.

The other alternative appeared to be even more difficult.

Who, he asked himself, among his acquaintances would be likely to employ as a governess for her children someone who looked like Selina?

Lovely young women were always a disturbing element in any house-hold and few of the Social Hostesses whom he knew intimately would be likely to tolerate an attractive rival to their own charms, however lowly her position.

"No," the Duke told himself, "it is not going to be easy!"

It was however not yet an urgent problem. In the meantime Selina must be clothed.

The order he gave Madame Françoise made her beam with satisfaction and curtsey half a dozen times before she left the Saloon.

She took the Duke's list, added a few more items with his approval, and promised that a number of gowns, shoes, hats, gloves, and unmentionable different items of underwear would be sent to the Villa as soon as she returned to her shop.

The rest of the order would be put in hand immediately. Tailors and seamstresses would work all night and as each item was completed it would be despatched.

She mentioned a riding-habit. She had one that she had brought from Paris as a model which would fit Selina to perfection!

It was naturally expensive but she knew the Duke would not quibble at the price when he had seen the young lady in it.

"It is a privilege to dress anyone so beautiful," Madame Françoise enthused. "With such a figure and with such a charming nature she is indeed, *Monsieur le Duc*, like Spring itself."

Madame Françoise and her *entourage* left the yacht.

Selina, wearing the blue gown, came into the Saloon. Now on her head she wore a little bonnet trimmed with ribbons the same colour and carried a pair of gloves in her hand.

"I am ready if you wish to go ashore," she said.

"We will go at once," the Duke answered. "I am impatient to show you my garden."

"And I am longing to see it," Selina answered.

She paused.

"There is something else I would like to visit, if you will not . . . think it a . . . bother."

"What is that?" he enquired.

"The Chapel of Ste. Dévote."

"Is it in Monte Carlo?" he enquired. "I have never heard of it."

"It is near here, just at the side of the harbour,"

Selina answered. "Ste. Dévote was, in fact, one of the first Christian visitors to Monte Carlo."

"How do you know this?" the Duke enquired.

"The story is among the legends of the Mediterranean which I read with Papa," Selina answered.

"Tell me what you know about Monaco," the Duke said.

"I expect you know," Selina answered, "that the Greeks believed that it was at Monaco that Hercules performed one of his twelve labours and carried off the apples from the dragon in the gardens of the Hesperides."

She paused to say shyly:

"I was thinking today that . . . you are like Hercules."

"Thank you," the Duke replied, "but I hope you have not eleven more tasks like the one you subjected me to last night!"

"You were successful," Selina said, "because you are so strong and . . . so magnificent."

The Duke did not reply and after a moment she asked nervously:

"Was it . . . wrong of me to say . . . that?"

"Not wrong," the Duke answered, "but most young women expect compliments as their right from a man; they do not flatter him in return."

"Why not . . . if it is the truth?" Selina asked.

The Duke could not find an answer.

How, he asked himself, could he explain to this inexperienced girl that other men would misinterpret her very sincerity?

"Go on with your stories," he said aloud. "Few people who frequent the Casino are interested in the history of the Principality."

"But it is such a wonderful one!" Selina protested. "It is where in 7 B.C. a gigantic statue of Augustus was erected on the heights of La Turbie to commemorate his final victory over the Gauls."

"Now I do remember that," the Duke exclaimed. "And I will take you to the ruins in La Turbie, which are directly above my Villa."

"Could we really do that?" Selina asked. "I would love to see them."

"After all these years they are still quite impressive," the Duke said. "The Romans built superbly."

He smiled at the excitement in her face, and said:

"You have still not told me who was Ste. Dévote."

"She came here in A.D. 300," Selina answered. "She lived in Corsica and was assassinated after she had become a Christian."

"There are as many Christian martyrs as there are gods around the Mediterranean," the Duke said dryly.

"The Priest who had converted Ste. Dévote," Selina went on, "planned to take her body by ship to Africa, but the ship was blown off course. In a dream he saw a white dove fly from the breast of the dead girl and settle in a narrow ravine."

"Which was here?" the Duke asked.

"The ravine is just where the town rises up from the Quay, Madame Françoise told me."

"So they built a Chapel there," the Duke said, anticipating the end of the story.

"When the Priest awoke," Selina explained, "the ship had landed on the beach of Monaco and above them, perched in the ravine, was a white dove."

"Then we will certainly look at the Chapel on our way to my Villa," the Duke said.

He could not help thinking that few people who came to Monte Carlo wished the first place they visited to be a Chapel of which he had never heard.

It was the Casino that drew them, the lure of gaming, the chance of making money.

They left the yacht and the Duke noticed how sweetly Selina thanked Gregson and the stewards for looking after her. She shook hands with Captain Barnett, who was waiting to see them off the gangway.

On the Quay was waiting the Duke's carriage with its pair of perfectly matching jet-black horses. A coachman and two footmen were in attendance.

One was on the box and one stood up behind when they were travelling but at the moment he was holding open the door for Selina to step in.

"The Chapel of Ste. Dévote," the Duke ordered as he followed her.

He could not help noticing that for once the footman's well-trained, impassive face expressed surprise.

It was a very short distance to where, overshadowed by the deep ravine which seemed to have been cut by a knife into the dark rock, stood the little white Chapel.

Just in front of it, with, the Duke felt, the secular callousness to be expected in Monte Carlo, there was high above their heads the railway line with which Françoise Blanc had connected Monte Carlo to Nice.

It was carried on by a huge brick bastion which almost excluded the Chapel from the road.

Once past the ugly brick-work the small Chapel looked like a white dove nestling at the foot of the rocks which rose above it.

Selina pushed open the door of the Chapel and entered.

Very little light penetrated through the stained-glass windows and inside was dim to the point of darkness save for the candles flickering in front of the Lady Chapel and the Sanctuary light hanging before the altar.

The place was empty and yet the Duke felt there was an atmosphere of sanctity which he had never expected to find in Monte Carlo.

Selina stood for a moment at the back of the Chapel, looking at the carved reredos and the statues.

Then she saw that beneath the altar was a marble statue of Ste. Dévote as she must have looked in death with the dove on her breast.

The Duke saw the delight in Selina's eyes. Then, moving forward, she knelt down in one of the old, oak-carved pews to say a prayer.

After a moment's hesitation the Duke joined her.

He did not kneel but he sat forward and bent his head, his eyes on Selina's face as she prayed.

Because he felt it obligatory and part of his duty occasionally when he was at Atherstone Castle he attended the village Church. When he was present he read the lessons.

He found himself thinking now of how his father and mother had attended Church every Sunday and that his mother had visited the private Chapel in the Castle frequently, if not every day.

He supposed it was still kept up as it had been.

He could not remember when he had last been inside it but now he felt that it was something that should be attended to immediately upon his return.

He knew, without being told, that Selina was thanking God that he had saved her from the Bordel in Algiers, and that it was something she would do every day in her prayers, not only instinctively but also because it was in her nature to be grateful.

She prayed for a long time and then when she sat back on the pew and turned her face to look at him he thought that there was something spiritual and shining in her eyes that had not been there before.

He rose to his feet and without speaking they walked down the small aisle.

When they reached the offertory box at the back of the Church Selina stopped and looked up at the Duke. He drew a note from his wallet, folded it, and put it though the slit in the box.

As they went out into the sunlight Selina said:

"I have nothing to give, but I have promised that from the very first money I make I will give a large thanks-offering to the Church nearest to where I am employed."

"I think your prayers express your feelings better than money," the Duke said.

"One must always try to be grateful," Selina replied. "Papa said once that if a man or woman gave us one tenth of the things that God gives us we should never cease expressing our thanks most volubly."

"I suppose that is true," the Duke agreed.

Selina gave a little sigh.

"We are so lucky, so very lucky. At least I am, because you were there to . . . save me."

"I told you not to think about it," the Duke said sharply.

"I still have to thank God for you," Selina replied almost reprovingly.

"Of course," he smiled.

They stepped back into the carriage.

Now as the horses started up the steep road which led past the Casino Selina had her first glimpse of the huge, white, ornate building which to many people symbolized the zenith of entertainment.

Ornate flower-beds laid out in intricate patterns filled the centre of the Square in front of it.

On one side was the Hôtel de Paris with its statues of half-naked goddesses supporting the second floor on their heads.

Rising up the hill were gardens with high trees, green lawns, and brilliant flowers.

Although it was still not yet noon exquisitely gowned lady visitors to Monte Carlo were moving down the steps from the Hotel and up the steps to the Casino.

Ospreys and feathers fluttered in their hats, fabulous jewels glittered on their gowns, and they were escorted by gentlemen as smart and elegant as themselves.

Selina looked at them. Then she seemed to shrink back against the cushions of the carriage.

The Duke felt her hand slip into his and she said in a low voice:

"You will . . . tell me if I . . . make . . . mistakes."

"There is no reason why you should do anything of the sort," the Duke answered, "but I thought that for a day or two at any rate we would stay quietly in the Villa. I want you to rest and take things very easy."

He felt the tension in her fingers relax and she replied:

"I would like that. I would like to be alone with you as we were yesterday. There is so much to talk about, so much I want you to tell me."

She paused and looked at him anxiously.

"It would not bore you?"

"I enjoyed myself yesterday more than I have done for a long time," the Duke answered.

He saw the gladness in her eyes.

He told himself that he spoke the truth even though

it surprised him and he knew how much more it would
surprise his friends.

He wondered for how long it would be possible to
live a solitary and isolated life in Monte Carlo. The
Social world would know that he had returned.

At the same time they knew how he liked to
organise and arrange his life. Neither here nor in London did people often dare to "drop in."

'I shall be firm,' he thought. 'Selina is tired although she does not show it, and my usual friends will
undoubtedly make her feel nervous.'

The horses were still climbing as he said:

"Listen to me, Selina."

She looked at him quickly, noting the change of
his tone.

"I am listening," she replied.

"No-one—I mean no-one," the Duke said, "must
know how we met or learn where you were taken in
Algiers."

Her eyes were on his as he went on:

"The story we will tell, and it is important that
we should both say the same, is that you have been
staying with friends in Algiers, but owing to illness it
was impossible for you to remain with them.

"As you are my Ward and there was no-one
available to chaperon you if you returned to England,
I brought you here in my yacht to stay at my Villa
with Mrs. Sherman."

"Surely no-one is likely to question me?" Selina
asked.

"People are insatiably curious," the Duke replied
dryly.

As he spoke he was well aware of the intense
curiosity and speculation which would be aroused
when it was learnt that he had returned with a young
and very beautiful girl.

He was determined to try to squash the gossip
from its very inception and he hoped that if he as-
serted that Selina was his Ward few people would be
likely to query it openly.

He had already before they had left the yacht
told the Captain that none of the crew was to mention

that she had been kidnapped when she was staying in Algiers.

He knew that when he gave an order his servants would be too frightened to disobey it. He made it clear to Captain Barnett that if anyone did offend they would immediately be dismissed.

Selina did not start to speak at once when he had finished, and then after a moment she said a little hesitantly:

"Will people really . . . believe that I am your . . . Ward? I am so . . . unimportant."

"It is not a question of importance," the Duke said. "Many years ago when I was at Oxford a friend and I, before we took part in a mad ride when we might easily have broken our necks, left a number of our possessions to each other."

The Duke smiled.

"My friend was in love with an attractive girl he afterwards married, but she was an orphan with very little money, and in his will he left her in my care."

"I suspect that was rather different," Selina said. "I am, of course, honoured to be your Ward and I am only wondering if people will think it . . . strange."

'They might easily think so,' the Duke thought.

At the same time they would not be able to prove otherwise and it would be a brave person who would challenge him on the matter.

"Leave everything to me," he said aloud. "I have told you to trust me, Selina."

"You know that is what I . . . want to . . . do," she said in a low voice.

She was still holding his hand and now her fingers tightened on his.

"I am beginning to learn that you are of very . . . great . . . importance but when we are alone I keep on . . . forgetting that you are a . . . Duke."

"I do not wish you to remember it," the Duke replied. "We are friends, Selina, that is really the only thing which need concern us."

She gave a little sigh.

"Yes, of course, and you will not . . . make me . . . leave you? Not . . . yet, will . . . you?"

"You shall stay with me until you feel yourself strong enough to travel to England, and when I have found you somewhere to go," he answered.

She smiled at him. Then he saw her eyes twinkle as she said almost mischievously:

"I hope you do not find . . . anywhere too . . . quickly."

The Duke laughed.

"I am beginning to think you are rather a minx."

"What is that?"

"A young woman who always gets her own way," he replied.

"Then I hope I am a minx," Selina smiled.

She looked away from him and out of the window and gave an exclamation.

"Look!" she cried. "Look at the view!"

They had been climbing all the time they had been talking and now they were high above the town and the road was lined with mimosa trees.

Below was the harbour and the great rocky promontory on which was silhouetted the Royal Palace.

Beyond again, stretching to the horizon, the Mediterranean was as blue as the Madonna's robe.

"It is so lovely," Selina cried. "I cannot believe it is real."

"Wait until you see the view from my garden," the Duke said with a touch of pride in his voice.

Two minutes later the carriage turned in through the gate, on either side of which was a high yew hedge, They drove up a short gravel path and then in front of them was the Villa.

It was white and almost Grecian in its simplicity, with Ionic pillars supporting the balcony which ran the whole length of the first floor.

The house seemed to glow like a jewel as they stood in the garden which had been the subject of more comment, more articles, and more newspaper coverage than any other garden on the Riviera.

The Duke's father had been forced to spend the last three years of his life in Monte Carlo because the bronchitis from which he suffered was unbearable in an English climate.

Feeling lost without the sport he enjoyed and the
Estates which he looked after and loved like a child,
he expended his energy in creating the garden of the
Villa d'Azur.

Strange, exotic plants were brought from all over
the world, azalias from the Himalayas, lilies from
China, orchids from Malaya, cactus from Mexico.

The result was breathtaking.

The army of gardeners who worked at the Villa
d'Azur tried to achieve what the Duke's father had
sought—perfection.

Selina stood looking round and, seeing the delight
on her face, the Duke drew her forward so that she
stood on a terrace looking out over the flowers and
the shrubs at the panoramic view.

"I think this should really be called Olympus,"
she said softly.

"Or perhaps Arcadia," the Duke answered.

"I cannot begin to say how marvellous it is!"

"Come inside and take off your bonnet," he suggested, "then I will take you round the garden, although it would be impossible to see it all in the short
time there is before luncheon."

"I could spend years and years looking at it!"

"Do you really intend to stay so long?" he teased.

She thought for a moment that she had been
presumptuous and then her eyes met his.

It seemed as though something strange passed between them, something that made her feel breathless,
as if she had been running hard.

The Duke broke the spell.

"Come along," he said, "I want you to meet Mrs.
Sherman."

If Selina had been apprehensive about her un-
known chaperon she was, as the Duke had expected,
completely captivated by the old lady the moment
they met.

With grey hair, but not in the least like the *grande
dame* Selina had been expecting, Doreen Sherman
even in her old age still personified the grace that she
had painted in her exquisite miniatures.

A thin, gazelle-like little woman with deep-set

eyes and sensitive features, she greeted Selina with charm that was inescapable.

Before they had been in each other's company more than a few minutes Selina was telling her about her father's music. It was artist meeting artist.

The Duke smiled as he watched them chattering away at luncheon, at which they had been joined by Colonel Grayson.

The Duke had had a word with his Comptroller alone before they went into the Dining-Room.

"You managed without difficulty to persuade my guests to leave?" he asked.

"Shall I just say I managed to persuade them, Your Grace," Colonel Grayson replied.

There was an expression in his eyes which told the Duke it had been far from easy.

"I hope you made them my deepest apologies. I realised afterwards I had been extremely rude."

"They were certainly surprised, but your wishes were, of course, a command," Colonel Grayson replied.

He saw that the Duke was waiting and so he went on:

"The Kenningtons have gone to stay with His Serene Highness. The Fitzgeralds to Lady Bristol."

The Duke was well aware that one name had not yet been spoken.

"Lady Millicent was a little difficult," Colonel Grayson said, "but eventually she moved to the Hôtel de Paris. I am sure Your Grace will receive the bill."

"Thank you, Grayson," the Duke said. "I realise it was not an easy assignment."

"No indeed, Your Grace," Colonel Grayson said dryly. "Will you be entertaining tonight?"

"Not for some days," the Duke replied. "My Ward has been staying with people who are ill and the experience has been rather exhausting. I wish her to be quiet, and this is originally what I intended for myself when I decided to come to Monte Carlo."

"I quite understand, Your Grace."

It was difficult, however, as they chatted away at luncheon, to think that Selina was tired or in need of rest.

With the buoyancy of youth she seemed, the Duke thought, to have cast away not only any feeling of exhaustion but also of nervousness.

She was completely at ease with Mrs. Sherman and, as the Duke well knew, happy to be with him.

She seemed to glow almost as if she were lit by a light inside.

As the meal finished the Duke said:

"If you do not think you will be too tired I thought you might like to ride a little later in the afternoon. I usually exercise my horses at that time, and if it would not be too exhausting to climb the hill above us I could show you La Turbie."

"Could we really do that?" Selina asked excitedly.

Then an expression of dismay crossed her face.

"But I have no habit."

"I have ordered you one," the Duke answered. "It will be here by then."

"It would be a wonderful thing for us to do together," Selina said.

"There was a condition to my invitation," the Duke said.

"What is that?" Selina asked a little nervously.

"That you should rest after luncheon," the Duke replied. "It is what most people do in Monte Carlo. Mrs. Sherman always lies down. And I expect Colonel Grayson does so too!"

He smiled.

"He always tells me, however, that his desk is piled too high with papers for him to have a moment's rest."

Colonel Grayson laughed but did not contradict him.

"I therefore suggest, Selina," the Duke continued, "that you have your rest in the garden. There is a place under the trees where couches will be put for us. We can look at the view and perhaps sleep."

"I would love that," Selina said and her eyes were like stars.

Colonel Grayson was used to seeing women look at his employer emotionally, but he thought he had never seen anyone look at him with a radiance that seemed almost unearthly.

'Could this child, for she is little more, mean anything to His Grace?' he wondered to himself.

Then he decided that it was impossible. She was too young and unsophisticated. It was not the Duke's way to take an interest in women who were not Cosmopolitan in their outlook, not a part of the smart, spoilt International Set in which he moved.

He was, however, like a magnet attracting every sort and type of person, a great number of them being nothing more than hangers-on.

It was unlikely, Colonel Grayson told himself, that Miss Gretton was anything but a passing fancy of whom the Duke would soon tire. In which case, unless he was very much mistaken, the girl would be left with a broken heart.

He thought it a pity and then decided that it was none of his business.

He had long learnt not to involve himself in the Duke's affairs, except those which concerned him as Secretary and Comptroller.

The Duke and Selina crossed the velvet lawns where, as he had promised, the couches had been arranged in the shade of several mimosa trees, against the wall covered in bougainvillaea, vividly purple in the sunshine.

Selina stretched herself out against the silk cushions.

The view below them with the sun shining on the waves seemed to become more dazzling every second.

"How can you be anything but happy here!"

It was a statement, not a question.

"Unfortunately people can be unhappy standing on the steps of the Acropolis," the Duke answered, "and happy in a dingy garret with only a packing-case for furniture."

"I knew that," Selina said, "but I did not expect you . . ."

She stopped, realising that the rest of the sentence might seem rude.

"I am not entirely insensitive, Selina."

"I know . . . that."

"I expected that you would understand me better than to think otherwise."

She flushed because she thought he rebuked her.

"I do!" she answered. "And I believe that beauty is a gift of the gods! Only someone who is blind could fail to appreciate this."

"I have a feeling," the Duke said slowly, "that it often happens in life that the small things, those that are closest to us, become great in importance and we forget to look beyond them!"

"That is true," Selina agreed. "And sometimes it is the small things in life that hurt most."

She gave a little laugh.

"Like pricking your finger. It is always more painful than a heavy blow."

"That is why so many people are unhappy and frustrated," the Duke said. "The life of the average person is made up of ordinary and commonplace events."

He spoke as if he was thinking out what he was saying for himself.

"Mama used to say that little things like good manners and kindness are very important, and saying something nice to everyone you met was like giving them a bunch of flowers," Selina said. "So many people live in a kind of Sahara Desert. It makes their life very dry and dull so that they long for the flowers of which they are deprived."

The Duke was silent.

He was thinking once again that this was the sort of conversation he might have had with Nicholas Vlastov, and he would never have expected to take part in it with a girl of eighteen.

He lay thinking a long while and then realised that he must have dozed a little. When he opened his eyes Selina was asleep.

She looked as she had the first night when he had gone to her cabin.

Her lashes were dark against her cheeks and she

had pillowed her face on both her hands, turning her head sideways towards him. He was certain that she had done so in order to look at him.

"I must be careful," he told himself. "Whatever happens, she must not fall in love with me so that I might hurt her. She has been through enough already."

At the same time he reassured himself by thinking that Selina had shown no sign that her heart was involved where he was concerned.

He recalled the manner in which she had lain her head against his shoulder last night, trustingly like a child. She had slipped her hand in his this morning when she asked him to tell her if she made a mistake. It was the unthinking gesture of a girl towards an older and wiser man.

He felt as if he could still feel her fingers in his.

She was sensitive and vulnerable and she clung to him because she knew that he would protect her from all that made her afraid.

"What the devil am I to do about her future?" he asked himself.

And then was afraid of the answer.

Two horses were brought to the front of the house at half past three, which made Selina exclaim with delight when she saw them.

She had come downstairs from her room wearing the deep-rose velvet riding-habit which Madame Françoise had delivered as she had promised.

It fitted her to perfection, accentuating her small waist, and it was fashionably frogged with white braid. With it she wore a white muslin blouse with a frill round the neck terminating with a small bow of pink velvet ribbon.

A high hat was, the Duke knew, the very latest fashion amongst the ladies who rode in the Bois in Paris, and it was encircled with a rose gauze veil which hung down behind.

"I have never seen such wonderful horses!" Selina exclaimed, looking at the chestnut that she was to ride and the black stallion which she knew was for the Duke.

"I have had them about a year," the Duke said. "I have ridden them in London and at Atherstone. I thought it was time they too had a visit to the South of France!"

Selina laughed.

"I am sure they are enjoying themselves."

Ignoring the groom who was waiting to help Selina, the Duke lifted her into the saddle and arranged the full skirt of her riding-habit.

Then, as she gathered up the reins, he mounted his own horse and they set off, climbing up the hill-side behind the Villa which rose steeply, so the horses had to take their time.

As they went Selina kept turning round to look back at the view below.

"If anyone had told me a month ago that I should be here, seeing places of which Papa and I had often talked, I would have thought they were deranged."

She gave a little sigh.

"Think of the people who have climbed up here before. Gallic, Roman, Greek, besides the Saracens and Moors."

"If I had known you were coming to stay with me I would have rubbed up my history," the Duke said.

"Would it be possible to find some books about it?" Selina asked. "Now that I am here there is so much I want to learn."

"We will send Colonel Grayson to the book-sellers in Nice," the Duke replied, "and also the Libraries. I am certain we can find there all the knowledge you require."

"Are you sure it will not be too much trouble?" Selina asked.

"Colonel Grayson is quite used to being put to a great deal of trouble," the Duke answered. "You are quite right, Selina, we must learn every detail about the history of Monaco."

He told himself that here was a blind spot where his aim for perfection had failed.

He always prided himself that he thought of every-thing. Yet he had to admit that while he had a vague idea of the historical background of Monaco, he would certainly like to look up many facts before he related them to Selina.

They climbed until suddenly above them they saw founded on a great rock the marble pillars, broken but still amazingly beautiful, that had been built at La Turbie by the Romans.

"It is a pity there is not much left to see," the Duke said as they stared at the ruins which were now surrounded by small, ramshackle houses, poor and dilapidated, obviously occupied only by peasants.

It was then that Selina turned and saw that to the North, far away in the distance, there were mountains and asked:

"What are those?"

"Part of the Alps."

"Can I see them?"

They were now on the top Corniche, which had originally been the only road to Monte Carlo. It was now neglected by the traffic which could travel along the new road which bordered the sea and which had made the journey to the Casino easy for the inhabitants of Nice.

"We can go a little way along here," the Duke replied. "But be careful of stones. As you see, the road is rough."

However, they found a place where they could gallop and where, when they pulled their horses to a stand-still, they had a far better view of the snow-capped Alps.

They were far away but in the light of the setting sun they looked magnificent.

"How I would like to see them near to," Selina sighed.

"It would be possible," the Duke replied. "But if we drove that far we should have to stay the night. It would be cold because it is still early in the year to be near the snow."

He paused, then said:

"That reminds me, soon the sun will be down and it will be quite chilly. I think it is time we returned."

"Must we go back?" Selina asked in a low voice.

She knew that this was an enchantment. When they were alone she could listen to his deep voice, hear what he had to say, knowing that they would not be interrupted.

"We will ride tomorrow," he said. "I think you have done enough for today."

"I am not tired," she protested.

"I am taking you home," he said firmly. "As it is we have come further than I had intended."

They rode back, Selina turning her head to look at the Alps, and the countryside below them which was undulating and covered with woodland.

She longed to explore it.

Occasionally she could see the spire of a Church and some buildings clustered on what appeared to be a little hill.

"It is all fascinating," she said. "Promise you will bring me here again?"

"I promise," the Duke answered. "But perhaps when you get to know Monte Carlo better all you will want to see is the green baize tables."

"I am not likely to become a gambler with no money!" Selina laughed.

In other women he would have known it was an invitation for him to remedy the deficiency, but he knew better than to embarrass Selina by suggesting it.

"I would like to go right along the coast into Italy," she went on. "I have always wanted to see Italy, and Monte Carlo is almost on the border, is it not?"

"It is," the Duke replied. "But as the road is not good it would be best if we went there by yacht."

"Oh, please . . . please let us do that!" Selina begged.

Then the Duke said:

"Come on. I believe you are deliberately dawdling. I want to get you home. I can feel already there is a chill in the wind."

"Yes, you are right," she agreed.

They put their horses into a trot. Then as they came towards La Turbie they saw in front of them a band of men.

They were heavily built, roughly dressed peasants, and at first the Duke thought that they must be leaving the village and going home after their work.

Then as they rode nearer he realised, with some surprise, that the men were spread across the road with the intention of stopping them.

He rode on, determined to pass through them.

"Be careful of my horse," he said in French.

Still they did not move out of his way.

Then, astonishingly, so swiftly that he was taken by surprise, two men took his horse's bridle and two took Selina's.

"What is it? What do you want?" the Duke enquired sharply.

"You are our prisoners, *Monsieur*," one of the men replied. "And what we want is money."

Chapter Six

Speaking in French, the Duke expostulated strongly with the peasants.

"I will give you what money I have on me but, as you well know, this practise of holding up travellers is strongly condemned both by the Police and by the Magistrates. You will find yourselves in serious trouble for behaving in such a manner."

The peasants did not answer but simply started to walk forward, leading the Duke's horse and Selina's.

"Let go of my bridle!" the Duke ordered.

He wondered whether he should use his whip on the two men holding his horse and thought that if he did so he could quite easily free himself and get away from them.

But it was unlikely that he would be able to free Selina at the same time.

"Where are we going?" he asked after a moment when he realised that they did not intend to reply to what he said first.

The older man who answered was, the Duke thought, their leader. He looked the roughest of the lot, with shifty eyes and a broken nose.

"We are taking you somewhere, *Monsieur,*" he said, "where you can write to your friends for the ransom we intend to have for you."

"A ransom?"

The Duke had thought that these men were no more than petty robbers who had been known to frequent the Upper Corniche road for many years.

They had, when the Casino was first built, been a constant hazard to visitors from Nice. But their tactics had been those of ordinary highwaymen.

Brigands, robbers, bandits, footpads, they had all

been known to operate in and round every town on the Riviera in the past.

But the Duke had not heard anything about them for some years and he had thought they must have ceased to exist.

"You must, *Monsieur,* be worth a good sum," one of the other peasants remarked. "And the pretty lady a great deal more!"

There was some rough laughter at this and one of the men said something in a low voice which fortunately Selina did not hear but which made the Duke grip the handle of his riding-whip.

He was well aware that they were in an uncomfortable if not dangerous position. It was unlikely that they would be able to obtain help from any passing travellers so high up the mountain at this hour of the day.

Already the sun was sinking in crimson glory and it would not be long before a swift twilight was followed by the dark.

The Duke could not see how he could circumvent the bandits' plan without involving Selina in a fight.

The mere fact that she was there tied his hands, and he thought to himself that the only possible course was for the moment to acquiesce in their wishes.

La Turbie was now in sight but the Duke had little hope that there would be anyone in the small, impoverished village who would be likely to come to their assistance.

Meanwhile he knew that Selina must be frightened. He turned to look at her, forcing a smile to his lips as he said in English:

"Courage! You must not let them know that you are afraid of them!"

He saw the fear in her eyes but she sat her horse proudly and her chin went up as she replied:

"You are . . . with me, that is . . . all that . . . matters."

"We have been in worse situations," the Duke remarked.

They had almost reached the village when the men

leading the horses turned sideways down a narrow, dusty road.

It appeared to plunge straight down into a green valley, but after proceeding for perhaps fifty yards they turned to climb up the side of the hill along what was little more than a sheep track.

The men were talking amongst themselves and the Duke realised that they were arguing about the size of the ransom they should ask for him and Selina.

They were obviously not aware of his identity, which was some consolation.

At the same time he knew that whoever carried the ransom note to the Villa d'Azur would be likely to learn who was its owner.

They rode along the hillside for perhaps a quarter of a mile before they came to a building half hidden by trees and the Duke saw that it was a tumbled-down house which must have been abandoned for many years.

Half the roof had fallen in, the windows were boarded up, and the undergrowth was growing right up to the door.

The bandits drew the horses to a stand-still and the leader ordered:

"Get down, *Monsieur*."

"Suppose we come to terms immediately," the Duke suggested. "If you let us go you have my word of honour you will be paid. Several or all of you can come with me and you will receive the money as soon as I reach my house."

The Leader shook his head.

"I am not so foolish as that, *Monsieur*. Once down into the town you would set your servants or the Police on to us. You will remain our prisoners until we are paid and then we will release you."

There seemed no point in arguing and the Duke dismounted. He then walked to the side of Selina's horse and lifted her to the ground.

He felt her trembling and she kept very close to him as they were escorted into the house.

It must once have belonged to someone with money. There was a large room on the ground floor which must once have commanded a fine view over the valley.

The floor-boards had long rotted away so there was only the bare earth to stand on and the plaster had peeled from the walls.

Creepers had come in through cracks in the boarded-up windows to cling and spread themselves inside.

There was, however, a large fireplace at one end of the room and at an order from the Leader one of the men started to light a fire, picking up pieces of the wood that were scattered on the ground, and another man was told to fetch some more from outside.

From another part of the house a man produced two candle-lanterns and these were lit and hung on nails which protruded from the walls.

The Duke was certain that this was not the first time the bandits had used this particular place.

They appeared very much at ease and moved about with an assurance which told him that they were proceeding with a well-organised plan.

The Duke and Selina stood waiting while the preparations were being made. A man appeared with a packing-case, which he set down on the floor, while another produced a bottle of ink and a quill pen.

There was writing-paper of a cheap quality and when everything was set ready the Leader said to the Duke:

"Write, *Monsieur*, and make it clear that if we do not receive the money we require both you and the lady will suffer."

"How much do you want?" the Duke asked.

"Ten thousand francs."

The Duke raised his eye-brows. It was a large sum and he was surprised that the bandits should be so avaricious.

"Your horses are fine beasts, *Monsieur*," the Leader said, as if he realised what the Duke was thinking.

He looked at the Duke's cravat-pin and cuff-links.

"We shall also require your jewellery," he said, "your purse, and, of course, anything the lady has on her."

"She has nothing of any value," the Duke answered quickly.

When he spoke he felt Selina move a little closer to him.

"Except, of course, herself," one of the bandits remarked.

He was bold-eyed and swaggering. He was taller and darker-skinned than the other men and the Duke was certain that he did not belong to the mountains.

He doubtless came from Nice, as did the Leader.

It was more than likely that they had organised some local ne'er-do-wells into a gang. The thieves, cutthroats, and swindlers in Nice were well known for their predilection for every sort of crime.

"You really expect me to ask for ten thousand francs?" the Duke asked sharply.

"If you please, *Monsieur*," the Leader said with exaggerated politeness.

To write on the packing-case the Duke had to go down on one knee beside it.

The ink was thick but somehow he thought that he might manage to scribble a note to Colonel Grayson.

He was just starting the first word when the Leader said:

"Write in French, *Monsieur*. We wish to read what you have written."

The Duke hesitated for a moment and then did as he was told.

> Miss Gretton and I have been captured by some extremely unpleasant and greedy bandits. They demand a ransom of ten thousand francs. Kindly give the bearer of this note the sum so that we can return to the Villa with all possible speed.

He held up the note to the Leader.

"Does this meet with your approval?"

The writing was strong and upright and the Leader was obviously better educated than the rest and read it aloud.

"You are very complimentary, *Monsieur*," he said mockingly.

He put down the note on the packing-case.

"Sign it," he said. "And address it."

The Duke picked up the pen. He signed boldly, "Draco Atherstone."

This was a code which would tell Colonel Grayson to put into operation a plan he had organised several years earlier.

It had been at a time when in America a number of rich men had been held up at the point of a gun and forced to write cheques which were cashed before they were released.

As was usual for a Nobleman, the Duke signed his name ordinarily with one word—Atherstone. It was not correct to use a Christian name, but the majority of thieves did not know this.

When Colonel Grayson received a note signed "Draco Atherstone" the Duke knew that he would alert the Police, who would follow the bearer of it without interfering with him.

The Duke calculated that Colonel Grayson would tell the bearer that he must wait a short while for the money as there was not enough in the Villa. This would give him time both to collect the money and to get in touch with the Police.

The Duke was furious, although he took care not to show it, at having been caught off his guard and at the mercy of such men.

He minded not only for himself, he was extremely concerned about Selina.

On top of what she had already suffered in Algiers, it was intolerable that she should be frightened in France, where never before had the Duke been involved in any such a situation.

He folded the writing-paper, addressed it to Colonel Grayson at the Villa d'Azor, and handed it to the Leader.

"It will not be difficult for your messenger to find the Villa," he said. "The name is written on the gates. It is a hundred yards off the main road leading down to Monte Carlo, surrounded by a high yew hedge."

"I think I know it," the Leader answered. "Perhaps the ransom should have been higher."

As he spoke he handed the letter to the man who was obviously to be the messenger and he left the house.

"It is quite enough," the Duke answered. "I only hope you will all remain free long enough to enjoy it."

"We will see to that," the Leader answered. "If there is any trickery, if our messenger is held up, your body, *Monsieur,* is likely to be found at the bottom of a ravine due to an unfortunate accident."

There was venom in his voice.

The Duke merely looked him up and down and said curtly:

"While we are waiting this lady and I would prefer to be in another room alone. We are rather particular as to what company we keep."

"There is a room upstairs," one of the men said to the Leader, "where we have put prisoners before. They cannot get out of it. It has a good lock on the door."

"You will find it cold, *Monsieur,*" the Leader said mockingly, "but if that is what you prefer . . . !"

"It certainly is," the Duke replied contemptuously.

He took Selina by the arm and turned to the end of the room where he felt there must be a staircase leading to the upper floor.

As he did so the dark-skinned, swaggering man walked forward to stand in front of them.

"Let *Monsieur* go upstairs," he said, "but *M'mselle* can stay with us. She can warm herself by the fire and I can help her to do so."

He looked at Selina with his bold eyes as he spoke.

She gave a little murmur of fright and put out her hands to hold on to the Duke's arm.

"We go together!" he said sharply.

"Who says so?" the dark man enquired.

"If you want money," the Duke answered, "this should be enough for you."

As he spoke he drew his wallet from the inside of his coat and threw it down on the packing-case.

"There must be nearly five hundred francs there,"

he said. "And I imagine I have some loose change in my pockets."

He threw down half a dozen coins on top of the wallet. Two of them bounced off onto the floor, to be quickly pounced on by two of the other bandits.

"A gallant gesture!" the dark man said sneeringly. "What about your jewelery, *Monsieur?*"

"Of course!" the Duke answered. "It's yours."

He handed his cravat-pin not to the dark man but to the Leader, and then he removed his cuff-links, sapphires set in gold which were, Selina knew, very valuable.

"That certainly assures you a place upstairs, *Monsieur,*" the dark man said. "But what about *M'mselle?* What can she give us?"

"You have what you want and the ten thousand francs will be here later," the Duke said harshly. "Kindly show us the way upstairs."

"I still say *M'mselle* should stay with me," the dark man said.

His eyes met the Duke's and the challenge in them was unmistakable.

He was the type of man, the Duke knew, who wanted to show off to impress his fellows.

The Duke put his arm round Selina's shoulders.

"Come, there is no sense in standing here bandying words."

He started to walk away down the room but the dark man caught hold of Selina's wrist.

"I have already said that she stays," he said.

"Unhand her!"

There was a note in the Duke's voice which told Selina that he was very angry indeed.

"That is what I am saying to you, *Monsieur,*" the dark man replied.

Selina twisted her wrist but his hand was like a vise and she could not free herself.

Frantically she clung to the Duke.

This was like her nightmare, with hands going out to hold her and the knowledge that she could not escape.

The Duke released Selina and clenched his fist.

"Do you wish me to strike you?" he asked the dark man.

The other man's eyes seemed to light up.

"I will fight you, *Monsieur,*" he said. "I will fight you for the woman."

"Are you man enough to fight alone?" the Duke asked. "Or are all these canine friends of yours to be yapping at my heels at the same time?"

"I will fight you alone," the dark man said. "A fair fight."

"If it is," the Duke replied, "then I am prepared to agree."

The dark man smiled unpleasantly.

"A fight, *Monsieur,* on my terms with knives. As my friends know, I am the master of the knife."

Just for a moment the Duke hesitated.

He knew only too well what a fight with knives entailed. It was a sport for the lowest riff-raff in Marseilles and other sea-ports.

Two men, each armed with a knife in each hand, slashed and stabbed at each other until one was dead or mortally injured.

It was a method of fighting which the Police had tried to stamp out unsuccessfully both in France and in Italy.

The Duke made up his mind.

"I will fight you," he said, "but on condition you all give me your word of honour that no-one else will interfere. And that when I win the lady and I may proceed as we intended to another room."

"You will not win, *Monsieur,*" the dark man jeered.

"That is a point that has to be proved," the Duke replied.

He turned towards the other men.

"Do I have your word?"

As he looked round at their faces by the light of the fire and the candle-lanterns he thought that they were worried and apprehensive about the turn of events.

He was sure that he was right in thinking that all except the Leader, the man he was to fight, and perhaps one other were only local peasants.

They looked stolid and simple and had obviously been led astray by the greed of the outsiders.

They were required only to make a formidable show and to intimidate their victims by sheer numbers.

"I would just like to say," the Duke went on before anyone could speak, "that if I am murdered you will find it causes a great deal of trouble for you all. If I am merely wounded I will give you my word of honour, in return for yours, that on that count I will not prefer charges with the Police."

"If you are in a condition to do so," the dark man said venomously.

"As you say," the Duke answered.

He looked again at the men in the room and asked:

"Do you give me your word you will not interfere?"

They murmured their assent in voices that told him they were far from happy.

They had obviously in the past held terrified prisoners captive until the money demanded had been fetched from their homes. When released they had been too thankful to be at liberty again to make much fuss about it.

The Duke was determined that this gang should be brought to justice but this was not the moment to say so.

The dark man was giving directions for the others to clear the floor.

The pieces of wood and sticks that were lying about were picked up and thrown into the fire. More fuel was piled on the flames to make it leap higher.

The lanterns were placed opposite each other so that the maximum amount of light illuminated the centre, where they would fight.

"Please, you must . . . not do . . . this," Selina said in a low voice, holding on to the Duke's arm.

"I have to," he said. "That man is dangerous, as you well know."

"Perhaps it would be . . . better for me to do what he . . . asks," she murmured. "I would not have you . . . hurt."

The Duke looked down at her face.

"Do you mean that?"

"You know I . . . do," she answered.

She spoke quite calmly although he could see the terror in her eyes.

"Do not worry," he said gently. "Just trust me."

Her fingers reached out to find his.

"You are . . . strong," she said, "but knives are . . . sharp."

She had noticed while they were talking that four knives had been placed on the packing-case on which the Duke had written his note.

They were short, two-sided, pointed knives used by the apaches in Paris and by brawlers in shipping-ports.

The Duke knew them well. One thrust in a man's rib with real force and it was unlikely that he would live to tell the tale.

They were knives that stabbed pedestrians in alleys, they were the weapons of a vendetta, the weapons used in desolate Inns where travellers had valuable baggage.

As the Duke looked at them he was well aware that he was at a disadvantage.

He had never actually fought with a knife, and he had only once seen a genuine fight take place between two men who were equally proficient with them.

Calmly and almost dispassionately he sized up his opponent.

The dark man was not as tall as he was but he would be lighter on his feet and more wiry. Both were an advantage in a battle of knives.

Moreover, he was doubtless the terror of the side-streets of Nice, a bully amongst other criminals, and he had undoubtedly used his knives in gaining a reputation as a "Master."

The Duke removed his coat as the dark man pulled off his shirt.

He had a strongly muscled body, the Duke noted,

and he was tattooed on the chest and on the arms, which suggested that he had been a seaman at one time.

He would be a formidable opponent, there was no doubt about that.

The Duke handed his coat to Selina and then he removed first his cravat, then his fine muslin shirt.

His body was very white compared with the dark man's, but his muscles rippled beneath the skin, and owing to the regular exercise he took there was not a spare ounce of flesh on him.

Selina took his shirt from him and he looked down into her eyes, which were wide and frightened.

"Trust me," he said softly again.

He knew that she was past words, unable to say anything because her breath was constricted in her throat.

The packing-case had been removed and placed against the wall. She turned towards it and sat down, placing the Duke's shirt and coat on her lap.

She clasped her hands together and the Duke guessed that she was praying as he picked up one of the knives which had been stuck into the ground in a row.

The dark man chose one and the Duke picked up his second.

"I will tell you when you are to start," the Leader said.

"One moment," the Duke interrupted. "I have just realised that my riding-boots may slip on the floor and I see that my opponent has taken off his shoes."

The dark man laughed unpleasantly.

"I hoped you would not be aware of that until it was too late."

"I am sure you did," the Duke replied.

He moved towards Selina and sat down on the edge of the packing-case.

He held out his foot, almost insolently, to the man standing nearest to him and, as if bidden by an un-spoken command, the peasant pulled off first one boot and then the other.

"Thank you," the Duke said.

He was wearing socks on his feet and these he did not remove.

He walked back into the centre of the floor. Now he looked at his knives and clenching each firmly by the handle he raised them towards his opponent.

The dark man did the same and the Leader, after a moment's silence in which everyone seemed to hold his breath, gave them the word to start.

The two men moved forward a step, watching each other warily, their knives at shoulder level.

The Duke realised that the dark man was too experienced to rush in and that he was looking for an opening, waiting to draw the first blood.

It was a case of circling, trying to intimidate one's opponent, making a menacing gesture with one knife while using the other.

There was a certain amount of skill involved but in most cases the loser was the one who first lost his nerve.

The Duke took a step forward. The dark man retreated.

Quite unexpectedly he dashed at the Duke, struck at his heart, and the Duke only just managed to move out of the way in time.

The knife, however, touched the outside of his arm and drew blood.

Selina gave a little cry, then hastily suppressed it by putting her hand up to her lips.

"You were fortunate, *Monsieur*," the dark man sneered.

"Skillful is the right word," the Duke replied.

"Next time you will not be so lucky. *M'mselle* is very desirable."

There was something singularly unpleasant in the way he spoke and the Duke knew that now the man was trying to make him lose his temper.

It was an old trick and one in which he had doubtless excelled on previous occasions.

The dark man advanced towards the Duke again.

This time the Duke was too quick for him and stopped him in mid-air. Wrist to wrist they wrestled with each other and the dark man retreated.

"You have the luck of an amateur," he said. "I am a professional not only in fighting but in love. *M'mselle* will find me much more attractive than a cold-blooded Englishman who has ice in his veins."

The Duke did not reply.

He realised now that he was up against a man so conceited and pleased with himself that he had no doubts at all about winning.

He was showing off, playing to his audience, completely confident that he would be the victor.

The only fear the Duke felt was for Selina. Nothing mattered except to save her from the attention of this boastful Romeo who might terrify her literally out of her wits.

The dark man advanced upon him.

He struck with his right hand and the Duke parried, only just preventing the knife from piercing his chest.

Once again the Duke received a slight scratch which started to bleed. In fact he hardly felt the impact.

If only they were fighting with fists, he thought, he could give a decent account of himself, and then suddenly something stirred in his memory.

He remembered, years ago, when he had been in China, he had been taken to a Shaolin Temple where he was told that they had practised a certain form of fighting called Kung Fu.

It was the British Ambassador who had suggested that the Duke might like to see the ancient art which had been handed down for nearly three thousand years.

"The Japanese make a great fuss over their Ju-Jitsu," he told the Duke. "But that is only a development of the original Kung Fu which was known in China 200 B.C., when Chinese soldiers were trained to become super-men."

The Duke had been most interested and he had watched the monks fighting in a manner that he had never dreamt possible. Their strength was unbelievable.

He saw one monk let his opponents break their wrists against his iron-hard stomach.

Another smashed a man who opposed him straight through a door, tearing off the hinges.

He was told that it was done by will-power and that there were men who could use their fingers like a dagger—just to point at an opponent and knock him cold.

The monks whom the Duke watched had used not only their fists but their legs. They would kick a man in the chest and knock him down when he was least expecting it.

Their surprise attacks were something he had never envisaged being possible in boxing.

The Duke could only remain in that part of China long enough to have two lessons in what to him was a new art. When he returned to Europe he had not been able to find a single teacher with whom he could continue to practise Kung Fu.

Now the memory of what he had learnt came back to him.

He was only anxious in case his legs were too stiff, that he had forgotten how to kick as the monks had taught him, and to use his will to conquer as they did without bloodshed.

"Come on, chicken-hearted," the dark man was saying jeeringly.

He danced about on his toes, making exaggerated gestures towards the Duke, obviously to bewilder him.

"I am in a hurry, *Monsieur*. In a hurry to get my arms round the pretty *M'mselle*. To kiss her warm mouth, to arouse a fire in her eyes as you are unable to do. To hear her telling me how clever I am, for that is what she will say!"

The dark man made a stabbing gesture with his right hand prior to slipping in a thrust with his left.

Then as he did so the Duke acted.

He drew in his breath and kicked out his leg as the Shaolin monks had taught him.

He caught the dark man in the soft part of his body between the ribs and at that moment, because he willed it, his leg was like an iron bar.

The dark man fell backwards with a crash and as he fell the Duke was on top of him, standing on

each of his arms so that they were spread-eagled beneath him.

There was a cry of amazement from everyone in
the room. Then with his opponent prostrate and utterly helpless the Duke asked:

"You acknowledge that I am the victor? Is this
man defeated utterly and completely? Or shall I knife
him to make sure he does not oppose me again?"

The Leader came forward hastily.

"No, *Monsieur,* you are the victor. Do not hurt
him."

"I wonder if he would have been so generous to
me?" the Duke asked.

"Let him go, *Monsieur.* I beg of you," the Leader
pleaded. "He has been taught his lesson."

"He has indeed," the Duke answered, "and let this
be a lesson to you—all of you."

He looked round the room, still without moving.

The man beneath him was writhing with the pain
of the Duke's weight upon his arms.

"Is there anyone else here who would wish to fight
me?"

There was silence and the majority of men looked
away from him.

"Very well," the Duke said. "I look to you to
keep your word of honour. The lady and I will go upstairs and you can keep us imprisoned until the money
comes. None of you will interfere with us. Is that
clear?"

There was no answer and he added:

"I shall keep these two knives with me in case anyone should feel inclined to do so."

"We keep our word of honour, *Monsieur,*" the
Leader said hastily.

The Duke stepped off of the beaten man's arms,
who gave a groan and for the moment seemed in no
hurry to rise.

The knives he had held in his hands had fallen
to the ground as he no longer had the strength to hold
them.

The Duke walked across the room and picked up
his boots.

Selina, holding his coat and shirt, was waiting for him and he put an arm round her shoulders.

They followed the Leader, who took a candle-lantern from the wall to lead them up a rickety staircase, from which the banisters had broken away, to the floor above.

As far as the Duke could see, it was the only room in the whole building that was left intact.

He thought it had once been the main bed-room. It contained two windows, heavily boarded, one of which must have looked over the valley below and one sideways along the side of the hill.

The floor was dusty but the floor-boards were intact.

There was nothing else in the room and the Leader set down the lantern on what remained of a stone mantlepiece. It had been broken, perhaps deliberately, and there was only just enough of the shelf left to hold the lantern.

"You will be told, *Monsieur,* when the messenger returns," the Leader said.

He shut the door behind him and they heard the key turn in the lock.

The sound swept away the numbness which had made Selina feel that she could not speak all the time the Duke had been fighting.

She turned to him now and hid her face against his shoulder. Even as she did so she recollected that he had been wounded and drew herself away again.

She looked round as if to find somewhere on which to lay his clothes and then put them down on the floor.

"Your arm is bleeding," she said. "I must bind it up."

"It is only a scratch," the Duke said lightly.

"It could be dangerous if dirt got into it."

Selina drew her handkerchief from the pocket of her habit.

When she looked at the slash from the knife on the Duke's arm she gave an exclamation of horror.

It was deeper than she had thought and the blood had run down his arm until it was crimson right to the elbow.

"There is a handkerchief in the pocket of my coat," the Duke said.

Selina bent down to draw it out, then, putting her own handkerchief on the wound as a pad, she tied the Duke's over it.

"I am afraid it will do little," she said in a low voice, "except prevent dirt from getting into the wound. We can only hope the knife was clean."

"I am healthy," the Duke said, "and it will heal quickly."

The mark on the other arm was really only a scratch.

Selina still thought that it should be bandaged.

Picking up one of the knives and turning her back on the Duke, she hacked a strip of muslin from the crisp, white petticoat which Madame Françoise had delivered to the Villa only twenty minutes before she was ready to go riding.

She could not help feeling that it was terribly extravagant to use anything so elegant as a bandage, but what could be more important than to prevent the Duke's wound from festering?

He stood watching her with a faint smile on his lips as she tied the strip of muslin in place.

Almost immediately the blood oozed through it as it had through the handkerchiefs on his other arm.

"Do they hurt very much?" Selina asked.

"Very little," he answered. "At the moment I am far too pleased at having beaten that swine to think of anything else."

"It was so clever of you! More clever than I can ... possibly say," Selina said. "I was ... terrified."

"I told you to trust me," the Duke said with a smile.

At the same time what really pleased him was that he had won without unnecessary bloodshed.

He knew that the monks of the Shaolin Temple would have approved of that.

"Let me put on my clothes," he said, getting into his boots. "And then I want to have a look round this prison and see if there is a way of escape."

"Do you think we could get away?" Selina asked.

"That is one of the reasons why I was so insistent we should be alone," he said. "Apart from the fact that I had no intention of letting that cur go on looking at you."

"I am so sorry," Selina said in a low voice, "that I keep on . . . involving you in these . . . dangerous episodes."

"It is extraordinary," the Duke answered, as if teasing her, "that someone so small should have brought into my life so many momentous adventures in so short a space of time!"

"I am . . . sorry," Selina said again.

"Forget it," the Duke replied. "Now we must try to prevent these bandits from succeeding in their abominable scheme!"

He smiled.

"Not so much because I mind giving them the ten thousand francs, but because to do so will encourage them to treat other travellers in the same way."

"Yes, we must stop them," Selina agreed. "But how?"

She helped the Duke into his coat, noting that it hurt his badly gashed arm.

At the same time it was cold up in the empty room and she wished that they could have a fire.

The Duke turned towards the windows.

The one which looked over the valley appeared to him to be more heavily boarded than the other.

Either the owners or their workmen had hammered long strips of wood criss-cross over the windows with huge nails, which would, the Duke was well aware, take a lot of moving.

The other window at the side of the house did not look much easier.

Then once again he remembered the breathing he had been taught by the Shaolin monks.

Their instructions had succeeded once, why not again?

He stood in front of the side window, breathing in deeply, holding his breath as he had been taught to do and letting it out again.

He did it several times, feeling as he did so as if a new force entered his body.

Then he told himself that when he pulled at the nailed-up boards they would move beneath his hands.

It was not only the strength of his arms that was important but the power he was using with his mind.

He reached out, gripped a board, and pulled.

For a moment he thought it was immovable and then, so unexpectedly that it took him by surprise, the top nail gave.

It made a cracking sound as it did so and the Duke stopped still, listening in case those below had heard and might guess what he was doing.

But they were talking, their voices rising and falling evenly and undisturbed—a sound almost of waves upon the shore.

This left three more boards to be removed and the most difficult were those that had been nailed up outside. It was harder for the Duke to push than to pull.

It took him a little time but by exerting all his strength and because by now he was certain that he was using his will-power the right way the boards came away one by one.

He had to prevent those on the outside from falling to the ground because that would undoubtedly make a noise which would draw attention.

Finally the window was clear and he looked out.

Because the house was built up the side of a hill the drop was not such a long one as it would have been in the front.

"We will do exactly what we did in Algiers," he whispered to Selina.

She nodded and he knew that she had been holding her breath while he worked.

Then she whispered:

"You will catch me?"

"Of course," the Duke replied.

She had taken off her riding-hat and her hair was very golden in the light of the candle.

"When we get outside," he said, "we must move

away from here as quickly as possible. When they find we have gone they will come in search of us."

"Where shall we go?" she asked.

The Duke looked out of the window into the darkness.

"Perhaps up the mountain would be best."

"No! I have an idea!" Selina said. "When we turned off from the main road and I looked below into the valley I saw a Church."

"A Church?" the Duke questioned. "Are you sure?"

"Yes. Down amongst the green trees I could see its tower and it had a bell in it. I know it was a Church."

"Then that is where we will go," the Duke said.

"They will give us sanctuary. Anyone can ask for that."

"If the Church is in use," the Duke replied. "Anyway, that is decided, we will go down there."

He looked out again into the darkness.

Twilight was finished, the stars were coming out, and as he stood there a pale moon came from behind a cloud.

There was not much light but enough to help them avoid falling into a ravine or getting hopelessly entangled in the undergrowth.

There was a road, the Duke remembered. If it went down the valley it obviously went to the Church.

Without saying any more he swung himself over the window-sill, hung by his hands, and dropped.

Fortunately below the window there was a thick carpet of weeds grown up high over soft ground. Not only did they break the impact of his fall but they prevented him from making any noise.

He looked up.

Selina, a little hampered by the fullness of her skirt, was climbing out after him. He remembered that last time she had no clothes to impede her.

He reached up, held her slim ankles, and then as she let go he clasped her round the waist. A second later she was standing beside him.

"Good girl," he said almost beneath his breath.

Taking her by the hand, they started moving through the shrubs and trees that circled the house.

They had to run some way before finally they found the narrow, dusty road which twisted and turned down the hill towards the valley.

When they reached it the Duke looked below and saw, as Selina had told him, what appeared to be the outline of a Church.

It was too dark to see much and clouds kept passing across the moon, which made it even more difficult.

"Come on," the Duke said. "We had best not waste our time."

Even as he spoke they heard voices above them.

"They must have . . . discovered that we have . . . gone," Selina said in a frightened tone.

Without answering the Duke pulled her forward and they began to run down the road, the dust billowing out behind their feet as they went.

Now the voices became noisier. Men were shouting at one another.

The Duke was sure that the Leader was giving instructions for the men to spread out to search for them, and he knew that if he and Selina had not had a good start it would have been difficult for them to get away.

Even now the sure-footed men who were used to the hills would move quicker than they could, and he was finding his riding-boots a heavy incumbrance.

On and on they ran and then, when they were both panting and the voices behind seemed to be getting nearer and nearer, they saw a bridge spanning a ravine and on the other side of it was the Church.

It loomed up in the darkness, tall and square, and they fled towards it, conscious now that their pursuers must have seen them, for they were coming straight down the hillside, shouting to one another.

They were not far behind.

Chapter Seven

The Duke and Selina entered the Church and found that they were in a wide, square passage which obviously encircled the actual Chapel itself.

They could see their way by the light of the little candles lit in front of the shrine to the Virgin Mary.

As they hurried past it Selina noticed that the walls of the passage were covered with framed pictures, drawings, and letters.

But there was no time to do anything but hurry on, hearing behind them the heavy foot-steps and the voices of their pursuers.

They found the entrance to the Chapel and upon entering found that it was illuminated not only with candles in front of statues but also by the Sanctuary lamps over the altar.

Kneeling on the altar steps, they saw, was a Priest.

Hand in hand, the Duke and Selina hurried up the aisle and as they reached the Priest he rose and turned round to face them.

"We are being pursued, *Mon Père,*" the Duke said a trifle breathlessly, "by bandits who imprisoned us and are demanding a ransom. We ask your help."

The Priest seemed surprised and Selina thought he looked at them searchingly, as if for a moment doubting what they had said.

Then as he heard the foot-steps coming down the passage and Selina looked nervously over her shoulder he said:

"Quickly, hide here."

He went up to the altar, followed by Selina and the Duke, and pulled aside a curtain.

Without waiting for an explanation Selina slipped through it, followed by the Duke, and they found that they were in a small, empty recess behind the altar.

A faint light from the candles and the lamps percolated through a lattice-work, carved and gilded, so it was just possible for them to see each other, and with a little murmur of fear Selina turned and clung to the Duke.

Even as she did so they heard the bandits who were on their heels enter the Church.

They rushed in and then stood still just inside the entrance, looking round, doubtless searching the pews and behind the pillars for their prey.

Then the Duke and Selina heard the Priest's voice:

"What can I do for you, my children?" he asked in calm, level tones.

There was an embarrassed silence. Then they could hear the Priest walking slowly down the aisle towards the men.

"It is late for you to be out," he said. "You, Pierre, should be at home with your wife, who is expecting your fifth child. And you, Etienne, should be attending to your animals."

There was no reply from either of the men he had spoken to and he continued:

"Your mother, André, is concerned about your habit of staying out late when you have to be at work so early in the morning."

He paused and there was a stern note in his voice as he went on:

"Last time you three Gautiers went to prison I looked after your families. They would have been in dire straits if the Church had not helped them. Next time it is unlikely Notre Dame de Laghet will be so generous."

"We were grateful, Father," one of the men murmured.

"Then show your gratitude," the Priest answered sharply, "by keeping out of mischief."

He must have then looked at the other three men who were standing in the background; the man the Duke had thought to be the Leader, the swaggering Romeo, whom he had defeated, and the other, who looked very different from the men from the hills.

"I see three strangers," the Priest said, his tone grim. "They come from Nice to tempt and lead astray more simple folk who live in and round La Turbie. But I do not intend this to continue."

He paused before saying forcefully:

"Go back to where you belong! Leave my flock alone, and I shall make certain of it by speaking to *le Préfet de Police* in Monte Carlo and in Nice."

There was no reply and after a moment he said:

"That is all I have to say to you except one more thing: anything that has been stolen is to be put outside my door early tomorrow morning. Big or small, whatever it is, it must be returned."

He must have seen some dissatisfaction in the faces of some of those to whom he spoke because he continued, almost harshly:

"When your hands are clean I will hear your confessions. But until they are neither you nor your families are welcome in the Church of Notre Dame de Laghet."

One of the men said, and his voice had a note of anguish in it:

"Our families know nothing of this, *Mon Père.*"

"Then it would be a pity if you had to enlighten them," the Priest retorted, and went on:

"You, Pierre, have had great benefits from the Church. The Nuns have taught your children and your second son's leg was cured by what seemed to all of us a miracle. Are you so ungrateful? Can you dare to defy God's commandments after accepting his mercy?"

"No, *Mon Père.* No. I did not think."

"Then go home and think now," the Priest said sharply. "All of you."

There was the sound of men shuffling from the Chapel and the Priest must have gone with them.

They heard him saying a prayer as he walked down the passage towards the entrance.

Selina gave a deep sigh of relief which seemed to come from the very depths of her heart.

She knew now how frightened she had been.

She was well aware that if they had been caught

the men, angry at their escape, would undoubtedly have been very rough with them both.

However strong the Duke might be, it would have been impossible for him to fight so many men simultaneously.

But thanks to his strength and cleverness they had escaped!

She raised her face to look up at him, conscious that it would be very difficult to express her gratitude in words.

His arms were still round her and then, unexpectedly, almost as if it was a spontaneous gesture, without thought, his lips were on hers.

For a second she was conscious only of a feeling of surprise. Then a sensation so strange and so wonderful seemed to run through her that it was almost like a touch of the Divine.

She felt her lips tremble beneath his before suddenly they became soft and yielding.

She felt him draw her closer still and knew that their kiss was perfect and holy, a part of the sanctity of the Chapel and of God.

It was a wonder and a rapture that she had not known existed!

She felt as if the angels were singing and the saints were giving them their blessing, and that he swept her up into Heaven itself.

How long they remained close to each other in a glory beyond expression it was difficult to know.

Only when they heard the Priest returning as he came towards them up the aisle did the Duke raise his head and Selina was free.

She was trembling with the ecstasy he evoked in her and with an inarticulate little murmur she hid her face against his shoulder.

He held her without speaking and without moving.

Then the Priest drew aside the curtain through which they had entered the aperture behind the altar and said in a quiet voice:

"It is safe now. You can come out."

It seemed to Selina that she was swept back from

the sky to the world below, and yet the sanctity and wonder of what she had felt seemed still to envelop her like an aura of glory.

Automatically, hardly conscious of what she did, she moved back into the Chapel and the Duke followed her.

They walked down the altar steps into the Chancel.

"I am very grateful, *Mon Père,*" the Duke said. "I am the Duke of Atherstone and this is my Ward, Miss Selina Gretton. We were apprehended by those men on the high Corniche road."

"I can only regret that such things should have happened within my Parish," the Priest answered quietly.

"We would wish to return to Monte Carlo, where I have a Villa," the Duke said, "but unfortunately our horses were taken from us."

"They will be returned," the Priest replied. "In the meantime, may I offer you my hospitality, *Monsieur?* And the Nuns would be delighted to take care of *M'mselle.*"

"You are very kind," the Duke said.

"And could you see to His Grace's arm?" Selina asked the Priest. "He was wounded by a knife and we had no chance of cleaning it properly before we escaped."

"Everything shall be attended to," the Priest answered, "if you will follow me."

He walked towards the door and when he reached it he turned and genuflected to the altar and then led them out into the wide passage outside.

As they walked towards the entrance Selina asked:

"What are the pictures on the wall? I have never seen anything like them before in a Church."

"They are *Les Dieu Merci,*" the Priest answered, "a thanks-offering from people who have been saved from accidents thanks to the prayers and intercessions of Notre Dame de Laghet."

"*Dieu Merci?*" Selina queried. "Thanks to God?"

"Notre Dame de Laghet is famous for protecting

and saving those who pray to her for injuries of every sort."

"I have been coming to Monte Carlo for many years," the Duke interposed, "but I have never heard of this Church before."

"It has been here since 1656," the Priest answered. "But those who are obsessed by the Goddess of Chance often forget the God who directs our lives."

"That is true," the Duke agreed. "And today Miss Gretton introduced me to the Chapel of Ste. Dévote."

The Priest smiled.

"It is a very beautiful legend. And I would like, when you have time, to tell you some of the miracles which have been performed in answer to the prayers of those who believe in Notre Dame de Laghet."

"I would love to hear them," Selina said.

By this time they were walking down the steps of the Church into the dark outside.

She could not help looking a little nervously into the shadows, half afraid that the bandits might be waiting to pounce on them.

The Priest led them across a small square towards a house on the other side.

"This is my Presbytery," he said. "There are a number of Nuns in the adjoining Convent who are attached to the Church. They teach the children from the village, they heal the sick, and travel over a wide area bringing help to those who need it."

Inside the house was sparsely furnished but spotlessly clean. Everything, Selina thought, seemed to shine.

An elderly woman came into the room where they were standing.

"I have brought visitors, Madame Beauvais," the Priest said. "*Monsieur* will rest here in my guest-room. And perhaps you will be kind enough to escort *M'mselle* to the Convent. A Night-Sister will be on duty if the others have retired."

"Will you come with me, *M'mselle?*" Madame Beauvais asked.

Selina turned towards the Duke.

She looked up into his eyes and for a moment it was hard to speak because she could still feel the glory and wonder of his kiss. Then as he looked at her she knew that words were unnecessary.

They were close to each other in a manner which she could not describe.

She knew only that she now belonged to him, both with her body and her soul.

"You will have your arm seen to?" she asked in a low voice.

"I promise that I will do what you wish," he answered.

She felt as if their lips were saying one thing and their hearts something very different.

Then the Duke lifted her hand to his lips and she felt his mouth on her bare skin.

"Sleep well, Selina," he said. "You have no more reason to feel afraid."

"I am not," she answered.

She curtsied to the Priest.

"Bonsoir, Mon Père."

"Good night, my child, and God be with you," he answered.

Then she followed Madame Beauvais through a passage, across a court-yard, and into the door of another house, which Selina realised must be the Convent.

Here a sweet-faced Nun called Sister Bernadette took charge of her.

Selina explained what had happened and how they had sought sanctuary in the Church.

The Nun's eyes were full of concern.

"It must have been very frightening," she said. "These evil men come from Nice and corrupt our poor stupid boys in the village."

She made an exasperated sound before she continued:

"They do not even understand the risks they run. They just think it will be fun to make easy money, and if they are caught we are left to look after their heart-broken and starving families."

"Your Priest was very severe with them," Selina said. "But they obeyed him."

"Father Ancelin has earned the respect of everyone," Sister Bernadette replied, "and they are also afraid of him, which is a good thing."

She gave a little laugh and led Selina into a room in which there was a long, bare trestle table down the centre and stools at which obviously the Nuns sat to eat.

"I will fetch you some soup and some milk," she said, "as I feel sure you have missed your supper."

"I do not want to put you to any trouble," Selina protested.

"I am afraid our fare is frugal," Sister Bernadette said, "as we are a very poor community."

Selina could not help thinking of the richness and luxury which pervaded Monte Carlo.

She remembered the ladies leaving the Hôtel de Paris to go to the Casino, glittering with jewels, doubtless ready to expend large sums gambling at roulette or *chemin de fer*.

It seemed dreadfully wrong that none of them should think of or help the work that was going on only a few miles away amongst the poor peasants who would not themselves benefit however rich Monte Carlo might become.

As if she guessed her thoughts Sister Bernadette said:

"We are very happy here. Notre Dame de Laghet brings amazing blessings to all who visit her."

"Your Priest spoke of miracles," Selina said. "Do they really happen?"

"So many that you would not believe me if I told you about them," Sister Bernadette replied. "One day you must come and look at the drawings, the pictures, and the letters from people whose prayers have been answered and who wish to record what has happened to them in the only way they can."

The Sister fetched the soup, which she served to Selina in a wooden bowl and which she ate with a wooden spoon.

It tasted of herbs which Selina did not recognise, and was delicious, and with it there was a piece of dark, home-made bread which she knew was very nourishing.

She also drank the glass of milk that the Sister gave her.

She felt almost like a child having her supper before being put to bed by a kind Nanny.

Then Sister Bernadette took her into the smallest cell that Selina had ever imagined.

It had plain white-washed walls and a narrow pallet on which there was a pillow and a blanket.

There was a chair on which to put her clothes and one very small mat on the polished floor.

The only decoration was a large crucifix hanging above the bed.

"If there is anything else that you want," Sister Bernadette said, "you have only to come and find me. I am on night duty and therefore you must not feel you will disturb me in any way."

"Is there always someone awake at night?" Selina asked.

Sister Bernadette nodded her head.

"Sometimes people come to fetch us in cases of illness; our Priest wishes us to attend the dying. At other times there are travellers like yourself in trouble, or merely exhausted after a long journey so that they can go no further."

"I think it is very kind of you to help people in such a way."

"That is why we are here," Sister Bernadette said in her soft voice. "To help others as God helps us."

Alone in the cell, Selina undressed and got into bed. The mattress was very hard and if she had not kept on most of her underclothes she would have been cold.

But within herself was a warm glow of happiness because the Duke had kissed her.

When she shut her eyes in the darkness she could still feel his arms round her and the touch of his lips on hers.

She had never known that a kiss could be like that.

When he had touched her she had felt her whole being come alive. A Divine power had swept through her so that she was no longer human but part of the whole beauty and glory of Creation.

"This is love!" she told herself.

She knew now that she must have loved the Duke from the first moment she saw him, but she had not realised in her ignorance that it was love.

She knew only that when she first looked in his face when she stood practically naked in that evil house in Algiers she had known she could trust him.

She had thought at the time that it was because he was English that she had called on him to save her.

She knew now that it was because they had faced each other across eternity and her heart had gone out to him.

When he had come to the bed-room she had known deep within herself, even though she was still desperately afraid, that he would save her.

He had been sent by God in answer to her prayers.

If he had not come, if she had been left to the mercy of the Arab Sheiks, she still could not visualise the full horror of what might have occurred.

Yet she had been protected and she knew now, when the Duke kissed her in the Chapel, that it was God who had brought him to her, and that she had never really been alone.

"How foolish of me not to recognise that I loved him," Selina told herself when she thought of how happy she had been when they had spent the day amongst the islands.

She had known then that it had been a delight she had never experienced before to be with a man who talked to her as if she was an intelligent person, as her father had done.

A man who listened to what she had to say and who had seemed to her full of wisdom and an understanding she had never met before.

It was not perhaps surprising that she had not

recognised love even though it had been there within her heart.

The Duke was so important, so grand, so entirely different from any man she had ever known in her whole life that she had been very much in awe of him.

Then when she had awakened from a nightmare to find herself in his arms she had known that she must cling to him and never let him go.

Ever since then she had been afraid of the moment when she must say good-bye and he would send her back to England.

It was not only the fear of being alone; it was, she now knew, the fear of leaving him, perhaps never seeing him again.

"I love him! I love him!" she told herself. "I love everything about him."

It was not only, she thought, that he was so handsome or so strong, or that he wore his clothes with an elegance that she had not thought possible in a man who was so essentially masculine.

It was also because she knew that he had an understanding that could only belong to a man who was sensitive and receptive, just as her father had been.

He was, in fact, part of the music of life, of which she had always been very conscious.

She had felt when she looked at beauty, in a view, in flowers, in a picture, that there were no words to express it, but somewhere deep within herself was a melody translating what she saw into sound.

She was certain that if she told the Duke he would understand, just as he understood what the view from his Villa meant, the sunshine playing on the sea, and the flowers growing yellow, white, and purple amongst the soft green grass on an uninhabited island.

"I love him!" Selina whispered into the darkness.

She felt herself quiver at the thought that on the morrow they would be able to tell each other so.

She wanted to stay awake and keep on thinking about the Duke but she was very tired.

It was not only that it had been a long day; it

was that she had passed through so many different and strange emotions.

There had been the excitement of having new clothes, the nervousness she had felt when they had approached the Villa, and the terror evoked by the bandits!

Most of all, she had endured a helplessness which had been sheer agony when she had watched the Duke's fight against the boastful, bold-eyed bandit who wished to possess her.

She had felt then as if everything within her had been squeezed into a knot which was restricting her breathing.

It was like a dagger within her breast as she watched the Duke opposing the lewd man who mocked and jeered at him.

But the Duke had a confidence which seemed to fill the whole room, and which Selina knew affected the men watching, so that even before he actually defeated his adversary she saw an unwilling admiration in their eyes.

But it had been a torture to see the Duke's arm bleeding from the first thrust of his opponent.

It had been unbearable to think of those sharp, deadly knives cutting into his white body.

She had prayed then, frantic, jumbled, incoherent prayers, almost without words, just pleading with God to save him, and still she had not realised how much she loved him.

It was only when his lips touched hers that she knew that she belonged to him and had already given him herself completely and absolutely.

"I love you," she murmured as she fell asleep.

When the morning came Selina awoke to find the words still on her lips.

She was awakened by the sound of a bell ringing in the Convent.

She wondered if she should get up and then she thought that it must be the bell to arouse the Nuns to attend early Mass, and that she would only be a trouble to them so she had best stay where she was.

She fell asleep again and it was two hours later before she awoke to see a Sister peeping round the door.

"Are you awake, *M'mselle?*" she asked.

"Good morning," Selina answered sleepily.

"I am Sister Thérèse," the Sister said, "and if you will dress, *M'mselle,* there is some breakfast waiting for you in the Refectory."

"I will get up at once," Selina said. "I did wake when I heard a bell, but I am afraid I went back to sleep."

"Sister Bernadette told us you were asleep," Sister Thérèse answered. "She has now gone to her cell and she asked me to offer you her respects and to give you her blessing."

"Thank you," Selina replied.

The Nun brought her a basin and some cold water and she washed herself. When she had dressed she felt dismayed when she saw the damage the night's adventures had brought to her new habit.

There were tears in the pink velvet. It was stained by the undergrowth through which they had pushed their way and the thorn bushes had scratched the lovely material.

But nothing mattered, Selina thought, except that they were safe and the Duke was no longer in danger.

When she was ready she ate her breakfast quickly. It consisted only of fresh bread, a little goat's cheese, and a cup of weak coffee.

She could not help thinking what a contrast it was to the many succulent dishes which had been offered to her on the yacht and which the Duke considered an ordinary breakfast.

When she had finished Sister Thérèse took her back through the court-yard and into the Presbytery.

The Priest and the Duke were waiting in the room where she had left them the night before.

Selina curtsied. As she did so she lifted her eyes to the Duke and he saw the happiness in them.

"I hope you slept well," he said in his deep voice.

"I slept peacefully," Selina answered. "I must apologise if I have kept you waiting."

"It was important for you to rest," he said. "And now we are returning home."

She had a feeling that when he spoke the last word it had a special meaning in it.

"Are our horses here?" Selina asked.

"They were waiting outside this morning when we woke," the Duke answered, "tied to the railings. There was also my purse, with all my money in it, my cuff-links, and cravat-pin."

"Oh, I am glad!" Selina exclaimed.

"So am I," the Priest interposed, "and I suspect that the members of my flock who insulted you last night are extremely ashamed of themselves."

"I hope you will not be too hard on them."

"I shall be hard only on those who have no right to come here from Nice and teach my foolish boys the cut-throat methods that are so prevalent in that dissolute town."

There was a note of anger beneath his words and Selina knew that he was deeply perturbed that the men whom he looked on as children should be led astray.

"I am coming with you to Monte Carlo to speak to *le Préfet de Police*. I intend to do everything I can to prevent a re-occurrence of what happened to you last night."

"We are very grateful for your kindness to us," the Duke said. "I have never been quite certain that sanctuary when it was asked of the Church would be forthcoming, but now I have no further doubts."

"I am glad of that, Your Grace."

"That is why," the Duke continued, "I would wish to give as a thanks-offering to Notre Dame de Laghet, on behalf of myself and Miss Gretton, the same sum that would have been extracted from us by the bandits, had they been successful."

"Do you really mean that?" the Priest answered. "As you know, the ten thousand francs was placed in my letter-box this morning."

"I expected it would be," the Duke answered. "Your powers of leadership, *Mon Père,* are remarkable."

"I have it safely here for you," the Priest said. "I understand that the Police who followed the bearer from your Villa found the house in which you were imprisoned empty."

"I do not wish anyone in La Turbie to suffer for this escapade," the Duke said. "And my thanks-offering is, of course, for Notre Dame de Laghet. Perhaps one day Miss Gretton will do a drawing of our escape and let it hang amongst your other souvenirs."

"I feel I cannot . . . draw well . . . enough," Selina expostulated.

"Many of our artistic efforts are very primitive," the Priest answered, "but their effort comes from the fullness of their heart."

"Then I will certainly try," Selina promised.

"Now shall we go?" the Priest suggested. "I will escort you in safety to your Villa, and then I will ride on to *le Préfet de Police.*"

"We shall be honoured by your company, *Mon Père,*" the Duke said.

The horses outside seemed to have suffered very little from wherever they had spent the night.

The Duke lifted Selina into the saddle and then mounted himself.

They were obliged to go slowly because the Priest's horse was old and fat, but he was obviously used to the hills and travelling over rough roads and Selina was sure that Father Ancelin rode many miles every year.

It was a lovely day and the sun rising in the sky was warm on Selina's face and on her bare head.

She had left her hat behind in the upstairs room of the house before they escaped and she was now hatless.

But she saw more than once the Duke looking at her, and she was woman enough to be aware of the admiration in his eyes.

When they reached the Villa the Priest refused all offers of hospitality and they rode up the drive alone.

As they reached the front door and the grooms

came hurrying to the heads of their horses the Duke dismounted and lifted Selina from the saddle.

"Welcome home," he said softly as he did so.

She felt herself tremble because she was so near to him. But there was no chance for them to talk alone.

Colonel Grayson and Mrs. Sherman came hurrying out, exclaiming with delight at the sight of them, at the same moment wanting to hear everything that had happened.

"I have nearly been off my head with worry ever since I got the ransom note," Colonel Grayson said. "It was clever of Your Grace to remember that the difference in your signature would alert me."

"I hoped you would remember our previous arrangement," the Duke said.

"I should have been very remiss if I had forgotten it," Colonel Grayson replied.

They went into the Villa and then Selina went upstairs to change out of her habit and to have a bath.

It was delightful to lie in the soft, scented water with the sunshine coming through the windows and casting a golden glow over everything.

As she dressed she felt a rising sense of excitement because the Duke was waiting for her downstairs.

There was no chance to talk before luncheon because by the time she had changed the others were already waiting for her.

Selina had put on the green gown the Duke had bought for her from Madame Françoise and as she went into the Sitting-Room where the long windows opened on to the terraces she seemed part of the Spring foliage outside.

She also looked very young and fresh and there was a happiness radiating from her which seemed part of the sunshine.

Colonel Grayson wondered what had occurred to make her look even more beautiful than she had the day before.

Then he saw the expression in the Duke's eyes as they rested on Selina's face and told himself that what he had thought impossible had happened. His Grace was in love!

Luncheon was delicious and the Duke's recounting of their adventures made them sound almost more amusing than frightening.

At the same time Mrs. Sherman kept on exclaiming with something like horror at what they had endured.

"And you used Kung Fu?" Colonel Grayson asked incredulously as the Duke told how he had knocked down his opponent with his kick.

"I was worried in case I had grown too old and stiff to use my legs in the way the monks had taught me," the Duke said. "However, as Selina will confirm, it was very effective."

"It was incredible!" Selina exclaimed. "I think all the bandits thought you were a magician! They were utterly astonished when the man fell down as if he had been pole-axed."

"I am determined now to find a teacher who will continue my instruction," the Duke said. "After facing those knives last night I am quite certain that to be proficient at unarmed combat is more important than using offensive weapons."

They had finished luncheon and were still talking in the Dining-Room when a servant announced that the Doctor had arrived.

The Duke rose to his feet.

"I suppose I must let him look at my arms," he said. "Actually Selina and the Priest of Notre Dame de Laghet have prevented me from having anything but clean, wholesome wounds which will heal very quickly."

"I still think it is wise of you to see the Doctor," Colonel Grayson said.

"You have already bullied me into sending for him," the Duke replied good-humouredly. "I will take him upstairs."

He went from the room and Mrs. Sherman said she was going to lie down.

Selina walked through the open window out into the garden.

She wanted to go to the place where she and the Duke had rested the day before.

She had a feeling that this afternoon they would have very special and very intimate things to say to each other, and what could be a better background than the loveliness of the mimosa trees and the purple bougainvillaea on the red sun-kissed wall.

She did not however, lie down at once on the couch, but instead she stood leaning on the balustrade looking at the view.

'Could anything be more beautiful?' she wondered.

The sun on the sea, the misty haze over the horizon, the harbour with its white boats just below them.

Then she heard someone approach. She expected it would be the Duke and turned round with a smile on her face.

It was, however, not the Duke but a Lady. The most strikingly impressive one she had ever seen. Dressed in the very height of fashion—the jewels round her neck and in her ears were glittering in the sunshine.

The Lady advanced, and as she did so Selina realised that her face was almost contorted with anger.

"I heard you were here," the Lady said, "and I wanted to see what you were like. This peasant wench whom the Duke has picked up out of some dirty gutter!"

Selina gasped at the venom and vindictiveness in the sharp voice.

"I suppose that you know who I am?" the Lady continued. "But in case no-one has told you, I am Lady Millicent Wealdon, and the Duke has brought you here merely to annoy me because he and I had a quarrel."

Selina reached out her hand to hold on to the stone balustrade.

She could not understand what was happening nor why this Lady was speaking to her in such a manner.

Lady Millie looked her up and down in a way that was contemptuous and insulting.

"The Duke and I are to be married," she said. "That is the first thing you should understand. And the second is that your presence here is making him the talk and laughing-stock of all Monte Carlo."

"What do you mean?" Selina asked.

But the words were hardly audible.

"I mean," Lady Millie retorted, "that everyone has been told how you arrived in his yacht with nothing but your peasant-dress, before he decked you out like a Bird of Paradise."

She paused for a moment and then went on:

"He may be a Duke, he may be of great importance, but this sort of behaviour can only damage and belittle him in the eyes of the Social world."

Selina made a little inarticulate sound.

"There is no place for you here!" Lady Millie said furiously. "Go back to the gutters from which you came. Get out of his life and get out of mine! The mere sight of you makes me sick!"

She spoke so violently that Selina took a step backwards, almost as if she was afraid that Lady Millie would hit her.

Then as she looked into the beautiful, angry face she gave a little cry like an animal that has been hurt, and turning ran away through the trees.

She ran as she had run the night before, frantically and desperately, as swiftly as her feet would carry her!

Chapter Eight

The Duke came downstairs smiling.

The Doctor had already left earlier, hurrying off to another important patient.

He had been with the Duke longer than either of them had expected because the Doctor had considered that the wound inflicted by the bandit's knife was deep enough to require a stitch.

He applied it deftly and it had caused the Duke little pain; but by the time the arm had been bandaged, the other wound cleaned and also bandaged, a certain amount of time had elapsed.

As the Duke reached the hall, one of the footmen came forward to say in French:

"The Lady is waiting for you in the Salon, *Monsieur.*"

As he spoke he opened the door into the Sitting-Room.

It was a large, cool, very beautiful room and the Duke had brought some of his priceless pictures from Atherstone Castle to decorate the walls.

He entered and the flunkey closed the door behind him.

The sun was in his eyes as he walked towards the windows and seeing someone standing there and looking out at the view he assumed it was Selina.

Then as he drew nearer he saw that instead it was Lady Millie.

She turned and came towards him, her eyes glinting beneath dark lashes, her red lips curved provocatively.

"Draco!" she exclaimed. "How glad I am to see you!"

"I was not expecting you, Millie," the Duke replied.

This was not quite true because he had known that sooner or later she would come to the Villa and there would be inevitable explanations and probably a scene.

But he had hoped it would not be now, not at this particular moment when he wanted to be with Selina.

"You have been very unkind!" Lady Millie said in a soft voice. "But I forgive you because I have been so eagerly awaiting your return."

The Duke did not reply but walked towards the mantelpiece.

She followed him. Then, putting her hand on his arm, she said:

"Let us forget all this stupid misunderstanding. I love you, Draco, as you well know."

"I am sorry, Millie," he replied quietly.

"For your unkindness? So you should be, but I am generous enough to find a dozen excuses for you!"

"Not exactly for that," the Duke said, "although I admit I acted somewhat hastily in asking you to leave the Villa so quickly."

There was a silence. Then Lady Millie said:

"I can understand that you were incensed. Perhaps I was tactless. But we have known each other too long for either of us to take umbrage or to allow a foolish indiscretion to disrupt our happiness."

"I want to thank you for that happiness," the Duke answered. "We have had many enjoyable times together, Millie but we both have to face the fact that it is over."

"What do you mean—over?" Lady Millie asked, and now there was a sharp note in her voice.

The Duke was obviously searching for words and she went on:

"You cannot go on being angry with me, Draco! It is too ridiculous. I am well aware that you brought that peasant-girl here just to annoy me, but I do not think she will trouble either of us again."

"What do you mean by that?" the Duke exclaimed. "Selina is my Ward."

"That is a lie and we both know it," Lady Millie

retorted. "You do not suppose, Draco, that the whole of Monte Carlo is not talking about the fact that you brought her back in your yacht with nothing but her native dress to wear and decked her out like a peacock to pretend that she is your Ward."

"There is no pretence about it," the Duke said firmly. "She is my Ward."

Lady Millie laughed and it was not a pretty sound.

"You really expect me to believe that nonsense?" she asked. "But I refuse to discuss her. She has gone."

"Have you seen Selina?" the Duke asked. "I will not have you upsetting her!"

"If I have upset her it was only to be expected. I merely told her to return to the gutter from which she had come!"

She spoke vehemently. Then the expression on the Duke's face made her gasp.

"How dare you!" he stormed. "How dare you insult Selina? I always thought you were a stupid woman, Millie, but I did not know you were a cruel one. You will have frightened her."

"Frightened her?" Lady Millie echoed. "Does it really matter if a woman of that class is frightened? I can assure you, Draco, that strumpets can well take care of themselves."

With an effort the Duke controlled the words that rose to his lips. Then he said in the icy tone which he could use so effectively:

"There is nothing more for us to discuss. I am sorry that you should be so vindictive. It will be impossible for me to forgive you for what you have done, and I hope I never set eyes on you again."

"Draco!" There was no mistaking the sheer astonishment in Lady Millie's voice. "You cannot mean it! You cannot be speaking to me like this! I love you, Draco, and we are to be married, you know we are."

"I have never asked you to marry me, Millie," the Duke answered. "And I have no intention of ever doing so. You have insulted a guest under my roof, and you have frightened a child who does not understand there are women like you in the world. As I have already said, I hope I never see you again."

Lady Millie's hands went out as if to hold on to him but he walked away from her. He crossed the room and opened the door.

"Good-bye, Millie."

For a moment she did not move from the fire-place. Then she said:

"If you think you can get away with this you are very much mistaken. You may be a Duke and people may toady to you but they will also listen to what I have to say."

He stood waiting at the open door and she felt that her words had not reached him.

"If you imagine you can foist your mistress onto your more credulous friends you are very much mistaken," she went on. "I will see that she is ostracised, cut, and ignored by everybody, and you will make yourself more of a laughing-stock than you are already."

The Duke did not answer and she walked a little nearer to him.

"I hate you! Do you understand, Draco? I hate you! And I will make it my life's work to show you up as the cad you are. As for that little harlot, I will make sure that everyone knows who she is and where she comes from. Make no mistake about that!"

Still the Duke did not speak.

His eyes were on Lady Millie as she approached him, seeing the spite in her eyes, the hard, vindictive line of her mouth, the manner in which her whole body was trembling with her fury, and her venom.

He wondered how he could ever have been fond of her. How he could have considered, even for a moment, making her his wife?

The footman in the Hall, realising that the door was open, came forward.

"Show Her Ladyship to her carriage," the Duke said.

Without looking again at Lady Millie he walked across the Sitting-Room and out through the French window onto the terrace.

He stood looking at what he could see of the gardens, wondering where Selina could be.

Then as he heard the carriage drive away he went back into the house and up the stairs.

He was well aware how much Lady Millie would have frightened Selina and he thought that she might have gone to her bed-room and shut herself in, perhaps to cry.

He knocked on the door and when there was no answer he walked in.

Selina was not there but he saw on the chair, obviously left ready for her by the maid, a straw hat trimmed with wild flowers and green ribbons to match the dress she was wearing. Beside it was a pair of white gloves and a small white handbag.

'That means,' he thought with a sense of relief, 'that she will be somewhere in the garden.'

He ran down the stairs and out onto the lawns.

He went first to the place under the mimosa trees where they had rested the previous day and where he had expected Selina would be waiting for him this afternoon.

But she was not there and he saw that no-one had lain on the silk cushions.

He took a winding path which led further down into the gardens.

He had not gone far when he found two gardeners.

"*Bonjour, Monsieur le Duc,*" they said politely.

"Have you seen a young lady?" he asked. "*Mademoiselle* Gretton?"

"No, *Monsieur*. No-one has come this way and we have been working here since noon."

The Duke retraced his steps.

There was no other path down to the lower garden and now he walked through the trees, looking for the sight of the green gown Selina was wearing.

He walked on until he reached the gate to the road.

Here was another gardener raking smooth the gravel that had been disturbed by the horses and carriages which had passed up to the front door.

"Have you seen a young lady in a green gown in this part of the garden?" the Duke asked.

"Oui, Monsieur le Duc," the man replied. "It was some time ago. *M'mselle* ran past me and out onto the road."

"Onto the road!" the Duke exclaimed incredulously.

"Oui, Monsieur."

"Have you seen her come back?"

"No, *Monsieur,* and I have been here all afternoon."

The Duke hurried to the Villa.

He knew that if Selina had run away without her hat or her handbag she must have been panic-stricken by what Lady Millie had said to her.

As he reached the front door Colonel Grayson came out.

"Is anything the matter, Your Grace?" he asked.

"There is indeed," the Duke answered. "Lady Millie has upset Selina and driven her away."

"I was rather afraid when I was told Lady Millicent had arrived that something like this would happen," Colonel Grayson said.

"Where can Selina have gone?" the Duke asked.

There was a desperate note in his voice which his Comptroller had never heard before.

"Has she any friends?" Colonel Grayson asked. "Could she go home?"

"No, no. That is impossible," the Duke replied.

He put his hand up to his forehead as if he was trying to think.

As he did so he knew that here was another Herculean task! There seemed to be no end to them and he had a feeling that this was the supreme test.

He had saved Selina twice from the most desperate situations, and now to prove himself finally he had to find her. But where—where could she have gone?

She knew no-one in Monte Carlo and only he knew how impossible Colonel Grayson's suggestion was that she should have gone home.

She would be frightened. She would want above

all things to feel safe as he knew she felt safe with him.

'Could she be hiding somewhere?' he asked himself silently. 'Waiting for Lady Millie to leave?'

Then he knew with a perception that he would not have shown in the past that Selina would be thinking not of herself but of him.

Lady Millie had undoubtedly told her that her presence at the Villa was, in her own words, "making him a laughing-stock."

Because she loved him Selina would wish to protect him just as he had protected her.

"I have to find her—and quickly!" he said aloud to Colonel Grayson.

His Comptroller, looking at him, knew that he had never before seen the Duke so perturbed or anxious. No other woman had ever affected him in such a way.

"Order a carriage," the Duke said sharply, "and think—think, Grayson, where she can possibly have gone."

Colonel Grayson gave the order to a flunkey who ran off to the stables.

It was not many minutes before the carriage was at the door, for with the Duke's efficient organisation there were always grooms on duty and horses ready to be brought round at a few seconds' notice.

The Duke gave an exclamation.

"The Chapel of Ste. Dévote! That is where she has gone, I am sure."

He thought of the peace that had been there and how he had watched Selina praying.

"I should have known then," he told himself, "that there would be danger waiting for her in Monte Carlo."

She was too pure and too innocent for the crude, sophisticated world which valued only everything that was rich, luxurious, and costly, and had no interest in the spiritual qualities which Selina possessed.

Then the Duke had another thought and this time he was more certain that he had solved the problem.

"You go to the Chapel of Ste. Dévote, Grayson,

and see if she is there," he ordered. "But I have an even stronger feeling that she will go back to Notre Dame de Laghet, to the Nuns."

"On foot?" Colonel Grayson asked incredulously. "It must be at least three miles."

"That is where I am sure she will go," the Duke said positively.

"I will hurry to the Chapel of Ste. Dévote," Colonel Grayson said and, turning away, he gave another order to the Major-Domo.

As he did so the Duke's closed carriage in which he had brought Selina from the yacht to the Villa, which was now drawn by the same pair of black horses, came round from the stables.

They turned in the wide sweep and drew up opposite the Duke.

He stepped in just as he was, without waiting for his hat or stick.

"The road to La Turbie," he said to the footman.

The horses started off, the road twisting and turning. But they were climbing all the time.

The Duke sat forward on his seat, looking out of the open window. He was searching the hillside for the sight of the green gown.

They climbed higher and higher until they were only a short distance from La Turbie and the Duke thought he must after all be mistaken.

Selina had in fact gone to Ste. Dévote. Colonel Grayson would find her and bring her back.

Then just as he thought of turning back he saw her.

She must have walked very quickly, or perhaps run, to have come so far up the hillside.

He realised that, as he had expected, she had not stuck to the twisting road which made the route much longer but had climbed straight up from the Villa, following no doubt, the narrow sheep tracks so as to avoid the long, flower-filled grasses.

The Duke stopped the carriage, got out, and said to the coachman:

"You will have to go to the top to turn round. Do that and come back to me here."

"Very good, Your Grace."

The carriage moved away and the Duke waited.

He saw that Selina was climbing quite slowly and he guessed that she must be feeling exhausted.

Her head was bare and very golden in the sunshine. Her green dress seemed to blend with the Spring grass and the wild flowers.

'She is so young!' he thought.

Then he told himself that she was old and wise in all the things that mattered.

In the fundamental principles of life, in the things in which he had always believed but which had lain forgotten beneath the superficial Social veneer of the world in which he had chosen to live.

What a fool he had been to think that any of that mattered.

To have considered for one moment that he should marry someone like Lady Millie and that she could have given him any real happiness!

He could hear Selina's voice reciting as he had struggled to open the trap-door through which they would escape from the Bordel in Algiers.

She had been terrified and yet the words she had spoken seemed to echo in the Duke's mind like a perfect melody:

"A mind at peace with all the world,
    A heart whose love is innocent."

That was what she was offering him—a love that was pure and unspoilt. And he knew that through it he was blessed as few men were fortunate enough to be.

He watched, and now she had nearly reached the top of the steep hillside, where the little path which she was treading ended on the road.

Her head was bent and it was only as she finally took the last step that the Duke saw that she was crying.

He moved forward.

"Selina," he said in his deep voice.

She started and looked up at him.

She was blinded by her tears. They were running down her cheeks.

"My darling! My sweet!" he said. "How could you leave me?"

He put his arms round her.

She made an ineffective little movement as if to prevent him. But he pulled her closely against him so that she could hardly breathe and his lips were on hers.

He kissed her and with his kiss all the wonder and rapture she had felt behind the altar seemed to envelop her again.

She shut her eyes as if the sunshine was too golden and too wonderful to be borne, and she could only surrender herself to the glory of the Duke's touch.

Her lips were very soft and yielding beneath his.

Then the Duke was kissing her eyes, the tears from her cheeks, and again her mouth, frantically, desperately, like a man who thought he had lost the most precious thing in life.

Only as he heard the sound of the carriage returning did he raise his head, but he still kept his arms round Selina. When the horses drew up opposite them he lifted her into the carriage and got in beside her.

The footman shut the door and the horses started off, moving slowly down the steep road. For the first time Selina spoke:

"This is . . . very wrong," she said in a small voice. "I have to . . . go . . . away."

"Do you really think I could lose you?" the Duke asked. "You belong to me, you are mine, and I will never let you go."

"I . . . must," she faltered. "I am . . . harming you. They are . . . talking about . . . you."

"I thought you would be thinking of me," the Duke said. "Oh, my foolish little love! Does it matter what anyone says when we have something to share so precious, so wonderful, which they could not begin to understand?"

He felt her quiver against him and, putting his fingers under her chin, he turned her face up to his.

"I love you, my darling."

"But that . . . Lady said you . . . were going to . . . marry . . . her," Selina whispered.

The Duke held her a little closer.

"There is something I want to tell you," he said. "I have never—and this is the truth, Selina—never asked any woman to marry me. Never in my whole life."

Her eyes looked up into his and he added very softly:

"Will you marry me, my darling, for I cannot live without you?"

He saw a sudden radiance transform her face into a beauty that had something unearthly about it.

Then she turned it away from him.

"I am not . . . important enough. People will be . . . shocked that you should . . . marry me. But . . . perhaps I could . . . stay with you and . . . no-one would know . . . like . . . being in your . . . Harem."

The Duke gave a little laugh.

"My darling, my precious," he exclaimed. "Do you really think that would be possible even if I were to accept such a suggestion?"

He turned her face round once again so that she was looking at him.

"I want you with me always," he said. "Not secretly or hidden away, but with me as my wife, as my love, both by day and by night."

As he finished speaking his lips found hers and Selina felt that there was no need for words.

They belonged to each other. She was a part of him as he was a part of her. Not even a Marriage-Service could make them closer than they were already.

"I love . . . you," she whispered as his mouth set hers free. "I love . . . you until I cannot . . . think . . . anymore. I only . . . want to do what . . . you want."

"I told you to trust me," he said.

He realised with a sense of surprise that they were already back at the Villa.

As he helped Selina out she realised how dusty

her slippers were and that the grasses and the pollen from the flowers had marked the hem of her dress.

"I must go and change," she said.

"Do not be long," the Duke commanded.

She hurried up the stairs and a maid came to help her change.

She looked at herself in the mirror and was dismayed that her hair was untidy from the wind.

She did not realise that her eyes were shining with the ecstasy of her feelings and her lips were red and warm from the Duke's kisses.

When she ran down the stairs again she was wearing a white dress that had just arrived from Madame Françoise and because she was so happy she had taken a white rose from the flower-vase on her dressing table and put it in her hair.

The Duke was waiting for her in the Sitting-Room. As he turned to see her standing in the doorway he thought that no-one could look so young and be the embodiment of all purity and innocence.

Their eyes met and the Duke held out his arms.

Selina ran towards him and he held her closely against him.

"How could you have been so long?" he asked.

"It was less than ten minutes," she answered.

"I have waited for ten centuries," he said. "Perhaps that is the truth! I feel I have been waiting for you since the beginning of time."

He held her closer still and then he said:

"But now that I have found you I will never lose you again."

He kissed her until the room swung round her and she could not think but only feel a rapture which was beyond words. At length the Duke drew her to a sofa and said, his voice a little unsteady:

"I have been making plans, my darling. I hope you will agree with them."

"I will agree to . . . anything you . . . want," Selina answered. "But you are sure . . . quite . . . sure . . . ?"

There was no need to finish the sentence.

"I am sure," he said firmly, "that I want you more than I have ever wanted anything in my whole life before, and that we will never lose each other again."

He picked up her hand as he spoke and kissed it, his lips lingering on each of her small fingers and then on her soft palm.

He felt her quiver as a little thrill went through her and then he said:

"We must be sensible, at least for a minute or so. I am planning that we shall be married early tomorrow morning. First a Civil marriage in front of the Mayor, which is compulsory in France, and then, because I know it will please you, my darling, a quiet service in the English Church."

He heard Selina draw a deep breath of happiness. There was no need for her to answer him.

The Duke picked up a form that he had put down on the table when she had entered the room.

"I have to have a few particulars for the Mayor," he said. "So tell me, my precious, your father's full name."

"Francis Hubert Gretton," Selina answered.

"Your mother's maiden name?"

"Elizabeth Kirby."

The Duke wrote it down and Selina said hesitantly:

"Perhaps I should tell you that she was . . . 'the Honourable' . . . although she never . . . used it."

The Duke raised his head.

"Who was her father?" he asked after a moment's silence.

"Lord Kirby."

"Lord Kirby? Are you certain?"

"Yes, of course," Selina answered. "Mama did not talk about her parents very often, but she did tell me sometimes about her childhood in their big house near Huntingdon."

The Duke stared down at the piece of paper on which he had been writing and then he said:

"I can hardly credit it."

"Why, what is wrong?" Selina asked in a frightened voice.

"There is nothing wrong, my darling," he answered. "It is just that Lord Kirby—your grand-father —was my mother's first cousin. This means we are related. You are, in fact, in your present circumstances, my Ward."

As he spoke he realised that this was the answer to Lady Millie's vindictiveness and spite.

No-one would listen to anything she said about Selina once it was known that her grand-father was a Nobleman and that she was a relative of the Duke's mother.

He also was sure that once Selina was Duchess of Atherstone her Kirby relations would be only too pleased to acknowledge her and proclaim their connection with her.

It was not that it would make any difference at all to him. The Duke knew that he loved Selina so overwhelmingly that he would have married her if she had in fact come from the gutter, as Lady Millie intended to assert.

But for Selina her parentage would open every Social door and there would be no shadows on their happiness.

But the Duke thought that she would not understand and there was no point in explaining. Instead he looked at the radiance in her face as she said:

"I am so proud to think that I am actually related to you! How pleased Mama would be if she knew!"

"Perhaps she does," the Duke said gently.

It was a remark he would never have made a week ago but now he believed within himself that it was possible.

"I am sure she does," Selina agreed. "And I know you are just the . . . h-husband she would have chosen for me."

She blushed a little as she spoke and stammered over the word "husband."

The Duke rose to his feet.

"I am going to give this paper to Colonel Grayson, who already has my instructions," he said. "He will take it immediately to the Mayor, and will also arrange for the Church ceremony."

He smiled.

"And then we will talk about our honeymoon. Would you like to see the Isles of Greece? If we go there together in my yacht you will be able to recite Lord Byron's poems to me."

"That would be wonderful!" Selina exclaimed.

"Later I think we will go further," the Duke said. "Perhaps to India, in search of those Holy-men whom you are so eager to meet."

Selina gave a little cry of sheer happiness.

The Duke went to the door, handed the paper to a servant outside, and told him to take it to Colonel Grayson.

Then he came back to Selina.

He put out his hand, drew her to her feet and took her to the window. She leant her head against his shoulder and he could feel the happiness emanating from her.

He looked out at the sea as he said:

"My friend in Algiers told me I must reach towards the horizon, and beyond it there is always another. That is what we are going to do together, Selina."

"You know that all I want is to be with . . . you," she answered softly, "for you to teach me, to look after me, and . . . protect me. I am . . . frightened when I am . . . alone, but when I am with you the whole . . . universe is . . . mine."

"That is what I feel too," the Duke said. "My darling, you have given me so much, but most of all you have brought me a mind that is at peace with all the world."

He drew her still closer and his lips sought hers.

He felt her respond, knew that once again that strange, unbelievable rapture was theirs because they were touching each other, because they were man and woman united as one.

There was a fire behind the Duke's kiss, a fire that seemed to flicker also within Selina. He knew that it was not the passion which dies but a part of the creative force of God.

It was Divine. It was perfect. It was a wonder beyond wonders. It was, in truth, a love that was innocent.

ABOUT THE AUTHOR

BARBARA CARTLAND, the celebrated romantic author, historian, playwright, lecturer, political speaker and television personality, has now written over 150 books. Miss Cartland has had a number of historical books published and several biographical ones, including that of her brother, Major Ronald Cartland, who was the first Member of Parliament to be killed in the War. This book had a Foreword by Sir Winston Churchill.

In private life, Barbara Cartland, who is a Dame of the Order of St. John of Jerusalem, has fought for better conditions and salaries for Midwives and Nurses. As President of the Royal College of Midwives (Hertfordshire Branch), she has been invested with the first Badge of Office ever given in Great Britain, which was subscribed to by the Midwives themselves. She has also championed the cause for old people and founded the first Romany Gypsy Camp in the world.

Barbara Cartland is deeply interested in Vitamin Therapy and is President of the British National Association for Health.